the
Christmas
VISITOR

the *Christmas* VISITOR

an Amish Dreams on Prince Edward Island
Novella

AMY GROCHOWSKI

Ambassador International
GREENVILLE, SOUTH CAROLINA & BELFAST, NORTHERN IRELAND

www.ambassador-international.com

The Christmas Visitor

An Amish Dreams on Prince Edward Island Novella

© 2020 by Amy Grochowski

ISBN: 978-1-62020-726-0
eISBN: 978-1-62020-665-2

This is a work of fiction. Names, characters, and incidents are all products of the author's imagination or are used for fictional purposes. Any resemblance to actual events or persons, living or dead, is entirely coincidental. Any mentioned brand names, places, and trademarks remain the property of their respective owners, bear no association with the author or the publisher, and are used for fictional purposes only.

Cover Design & Typesetting by Hannah Nichols
Ebook Conversion by Anna Riebe Raats

AMBASSADOR INTERNATIONAL
Emerald House
411 University Ridge, Suite B14
Greenville, SC 29601, USA
www.ambassador-international.com

AMBASSADOR BOOKS
The Mount
2 Woodstock Link
Belfast, BT6 8DD, Northern Ireland, UK
www.ambassadormedia.co.uk

The colophon is a trademark of Ambassador, a Christian publishing company.

To Mom

For allowing God to write your love story

AUTHOR'S NOTE

The Christmas Visitor was written in a pre-COVID-19 world. In these last stages of editing before publication, I am acutely aware some scenes may no longer be plausible in the originally intended timeframe of Christmas 2020. If I were an author of science fiction, I may attempt to re-work the story into an image of what the future may be. However, as a lover of history, I have chosen to leave the story unchanged with the prayerful expectation of a world where travel and social gatherings will once again be safe and healthy every-day experiences.

Even the youths shall faint and be weary, and the young men shall utterly fall:

But they that wait upon the LORD shall renew their strength;

they shall mount up with wings as eagles;

they shall run, and not be weary; and they shall walk, and not faint.

Isaiah 40:30-31

CHAPTER ONE

After a long trek to the veterinarian's office, Mattie Beller was out of breath before she managed to push her scooter halfway up the steep hill to Annandale Farm. She inhaled as deeply as her burning lungs allowed, only to lose most of the precious fresh air to a hacking cough.

Like an invitation to step out of the cold and rest a spell, smoke wafted heavenward out of the new schoolhouse chimney. The children would have gone home hours ago, but their new teacher, Ellen Miller, must still be at work.

The urgent order of calcium supplements for the Yoder's jersey cow remained tucked safely in the basket attached to the front of her blue scooter. A visit with her new friend wouldn't delay her overlong and would give her a second wind before she made her delivery to the Yoder's farm—another two hundred yards up the hill.

Mattie crossed the road to the empty schoolyard and rested the scooter against the front porch. One surviving pansy, protected by the bottom step, sported a bright lavender bloom in defiance of the cold.

A shiver shimmied up her spine, although she couldn't decide whether it was against the early December chill or the reminder of her decision to reject the school board's offer.

She shook the nagging doubt from her thoughts.

Ellen was a *goot* teacher. Everything was surely working out for the best.

She eased the front door open in an effort not to startle Ellen. "Hello. It's only me."

"*Kumm rei.*" Ellen called for her to come inside. Her attention remained focused on her work at the desk. The pencil in her hand glided across the paper at the top of a stack, making an occasional mark. "*Vass kann ich du fa dich?*"

What can I do for you? Mattie laughed at the formality. Or she would have, except the sound stuck in her throat and turned into a squeaking cough.

Ellen dropped her pencil and came running to Mattie's side.

"Oh, Mattie! Are you all right? I thought you were one of the parents."

"Fine. Just need to catch my breath."

"Sit down." Ellen pulled out the chair from behind her desk, and Mattie didn't hesitate. She hadn't had a spell this bad for a long time. She'd had more than her fair share back in her school days. Thankfully, today she wouldn't endure the teasing she had back then.

"Better?" Ellen's kindness drew her back to the present.

"Very much. *Danki.*" The ache in her chest was lessening and each breath becoming easier. "I'm on my way from the vet with medicine for the Yoder's jersey cow. I saw you were still here."

"I'm so glad you stopped. I'd much rather a visit from you than from a parent. Not that I don't like them or anything. But a friendly visit is better."

"You know . . . I am on my way to the Yoders' house. I may have to tell our new minister about this." Mattie watched the horror on Ellen's face turn to understanding, and they burst into laughter at the same time.

"'A merry heart doeth good like a medicine,' like the Bible says, for sure. You're not coughing anymore, Mattie."

Nay, she wasn't. What a relief. Maybe she'd outgrow this horrible asthma after all. She'd hoped for that miracle when she turned eighteen. Two years later, she was still waiting.

"Now I've got my breath, I'd better get on up to the farm. Rachel was very worried that Joel might need it." And as a dairy farmer's daughter, Mattie understood Rachel's urgency. Mattie stood and returned the chair to the teacher's desk.

"I am sorry to see you go so soon." Ellen walked with her to the door. "I am sure if Rachel thinks the medicine is needed right away, then you must go. You know, I have never known an Amish woman who is a vet tech before. Our bishop and ministers would never allow such a thing; but I sure hope that if I never marry, I'll be as happy as Rachel."

Mattie was doubtful Ellen truly needed to worry over becoming a spinster. Mattie's twin brother, Mark, kept his business pretty close to the chest, but he'd sure been easier to get along with since Ellen came to the district to teach. Not to mention the long looks she'd seen pass between Ellen and Mark at every church gathering or the late nights Mark came home in the buggy after being gone for no reason.

"I suppose as long as we are doing whatever work *Gott* has given us, then we can be content." Mattie sure hoped so because if happiness depended on marriage, she was in trouble.

Even before her family moved to the island, where eligible men were few to none, Mattie had small hopes of attracting one. Rachel, on the other hand, was beautiful, and everyone loved her. She could be married, if she wanted, even if she had passed the typical marrying age. She'd told Mattie she was still waiting for the one *Gott* had for her. In the meantime, she meant to be about *Gott's* business, which for her was caring for animals. And for once, the future looked a little brighter to Mattie after that conversation. She only needed to find the work *Gott* had for her.

Mattie retrieved her scooter, not that she could ride it up the hill. She'd have to drag it alongside her. She looked over at Ellen standing on the front stoop. "Maybe I can come again soon and stay for a longer visit."

"I'd like that. If you weren't in a hurry, you could wait and catch a ride with me. My cousin is going to pick me up in an hour or so."

How strange. As far as Mattie knew, all of Ellen's kinfolk lived in the States, except for Lydia Yoder. Lydia was originally from Lancaster, Pennsylvania, and recommended Ellen for the teacher position after . . . since no one else was available.

How did a cousin all the way from Pennsylvania come for a visit to Prince Edward Island without Mattie ever hearing a word about it?

"So, your cousin is related to Lydia, as well? When Rachel sent me from the vet with this medicine, she never mentioned that anyone was visiting with the Yoders for Christmas."

"You know Rachel. She's always focused on her work with the animals. I guess she didn't think about it. My cousin isn't related to Lydia, but they were neighbors. And Lydia was our teacher for our first and second years of school."

Mattie still didn't understand how she had missed the news, but she did recall a neighbor of Lydia's who fit the description. A super shy girl who visited with Lydia's family at Christmas a few years ago. She'd helped Lydia's sister-in-law with the children.

Mattie hoped the girl had outgrown some of her shyness. Ever since her family moved to the island, Mattie had been lonely without her friends back in Ontario. How often had she longed for female company outside of married women or children? First Ellen and now . . . Anna. Was that her name? No matter. This Christmas might not be so gloomy after all.

"This is *wunderbaar goot* news, Ellen. New Hope has been lonely without other young people."

"Why don't you drop off the medicine and then go with us to town? I want to get a few small gifts to send home. Maybe the three of us can even go to a restaurant for supper."

Anna must have changed dramatically, if she was confident enough to drive a buggy to town. Mattie found such a remarkable change difficult to imagine. Ellen, however, was more than bold enough to do the driving.

"I'd want to make sure my *mamm* doesn't need me to help with supper at home tonight." Even if *Mamm* needed her, Mattie would welcome the ride home. She'd had enough exercise for the day already. But knowing *Mamm*, she'd shoo Mattie right out the door at an opportunity like this. "Would you mind stopping by my house to check? It's on the way."

"Of course not. When you get to the Yoders', just explain everything to, um, my cousin. I'll wait here for you both." The twinkle in Ellen's eyes and the drawl of her words as she referred to her cousin struck Mattie as odd.

Oh, well. She didn't know Ellen well enough to understand her peculiarities—a fact Mattie was eager to change. Probably not as much as Mark, though. Mattie couldn't help but smile. Mark deserved a special someone. And having a sister would be a pleasure among six brothers.

"*Ya,* Ellen. I'll hurry. We'll be back for you, right on time. *Danki* for the invitation."

"No need to rush. Take your time." Again, Ellen smiled with a little more mischief than the situation warranted.

Maybe she was hoping for a chance to see Mark. Mattie didn't mind. She was happy to finally have the kind of fun a single young woman ought to be enjoying with friends. Even the remainder of the hill to the Yoders' farm didn't appear quite so daunting now.

She reached the top of the hill a little less winded than when she'd gotten to the school. But she was increasingly thankful she'd be riding in a buggy after this. When she'd left home to run this errand for Rachel and the Yoders, she hadn't any hint her asthma would act up on her. But asthma never asked her permission to come a'courtin'. A more unwelcome suitor had never lived.

Ach, now Ellen Miller had her thinking in terms of beaus and matchmaking. And that kind of thinking was sure to lead Mattie to disappointment.

An open sign hung in the window of Lydia's Amish Shoppe, which occupied the side of the barn nearest the road. A visit in the shop to see Lydia and Anna first was tempting, but she really ought to go straight to the barn and deliver the supplements to Joel.

"Halloo?" Her voice echoed off the walls inside the barn. A whinny from Joel's Morgan mare, Amazon, was her only reply. The barn was immaculate, as she expected. She placed the calcium supplement package on a dry shelf next to the handwashing station. The milking stall appeared recently scrubbed and made ready for use again after the jersey calved. The adjoining stall smelled of fresh straw but lay empty as well.

Walking out the opposite end of the barn, she caught sight of the jersey lying on her side in a corner of the small fenced lot.

Mattie neared enough to observe the swollen udders but paused to avoid distracting the cow from her labor. "Poor girl, looks like today is the day, for sure."

The cow's pregnant belly squeezed with a contraction, and the animal kicked at her sides in protest. Rachel's sixth sense about animals sure did pay off. If the cow ended up needing the calcium after she calved, then Mattie had arrived just in time.

Where was Joel?

She slipped back through the barn and looked across the fields. Well, wherever he'd gone, he'd be back soon enough. After all, he'd been concerned enough to call the vet. Besides, she knew what to do. She was a dairy farmer's daughter, after all. It wasn't the old cow's first time at this either. If worse came to worse, she'd run get Lydia to find her husband.

She headed back through the barn and stopped to wash at the sink. Just in case. Her *datt* preached cleanliness in assisting a birth. She scrubbed all the way up to her elbows with disinfectant soap and rinsed well. As she reached for the paper towels, she sensed someone standing in the doorway.

"Not sure she's ready yet. I'm glad you're here, though. You probably have more experience in this sort of thing."

Have experience. Joel knew better. He must be joking.

She tossed the towel in the waste basket, found some lubricant and a glove on a shelf, then turned toward the door. Instead of her church's minister, a young Amish man with no hat and a mess of sun-streaked, brown hair leaned casually against the door post. *Who in the world are you?*

There were a few other church districts in the area, but the strict Troyer Amish church never mixed with hers. Besides, this man wasn't dressed as they did, and he didn't look like the more relaxed Mennonite church group either.

A warm merriment flickered in his dark brown eyes, as if he understood perfectly how he'd thrown her off balance.

"Where did you come from?" Her voice finally caught up with her.

"Pennsylvania." He pushed off the post and stepped closer to Mattie. "Sorry, I started us off on the wrong foot. I was coming back from telling Joel that Cowsy might be getting more distressed, and I saw you headed in here. I didn't mean to sneak up on you."

Cowsy?

"I'm Winston."

Winston—what a nice name. He was unusually handsome. He was also a stranger, who had called the old jersey *Cowsy* as if he was a child. But Mattie's thoughts were such a jumble, she couldn't be sure. Maybe she was the addled one.

He was looking at her. Those intense, brown eyes changing from warm to questioning.

"*Ach*, I'm Mattie." How she wished Joel would hurry and save her from this awkward encounter. "I was just delivering some calcium supplements. So, um . . . I—or we, I guess—should go check on her. The cow."

Winston stepped aside and motioned for her to go first. The gesture gave her a pleasant thrill, like the comfort of a silky sip of hot chocolate on a cold winter's day. She *was* the daft one.

Walking ahead of him, she couldn't help but look behind her and ask, "Did you say *Cowsy?*"

The answer came as a low rumble of laughter.

"Wait." She whirled around. "Are you Ellen's cousin?"

The cute Amish woman came to a sudden stop and turned on a dime.

Winston stumbled back a step to avoid plowing right into her. Her eyes, the deep blue of a dusky sky, were pinned straight at him.

He might not dare confess to being Ellen's cousin.

First, she'd seemed unsure of him, as if he was the child who'd named the jersey *Cowsy.* Seven-year-old Samy Yoder insisted he call her beloved animal by name. He thought it was cute until he made a fool out of himself. And now, the pretty young woman was giving him a hard, questioning look, as if he wasn't who he claimed to be.

"I am. We're first cousins." He had no reason to lie about it.

Mattie's apron caught a breeze and billowed out from under the hand she'd planted firmly on her hip. Her lower lip pouted ever so slightly, and her eyes dimmed further as she cast her look downward. A prayer *kapp* covered her light brown curls—mostly. Small ringlets escaped their confinement at her temples. More appeared along the back of her neck when she turned and stalked toward the laboring cow.

The woman was as alluring as she was confusing. Winston didn't consider himself a difficult person. He got along with almost anyone, but Mattie was already proving a challenge.

Ellen had told him about Mattie. She was one of only two unmarried Amish females over the age of sixteen in the New Hope church district. Rachel was the other, and she had no interest in marriage. Or so Ellen said.

By the reception he received just now, he had to wonder what his cousin was up to. She either hadn't mentioned him to her new friend, or her description had put Mattie off. Of course, it made no difference to him. She had nothing to do with his reasons for coming to this new church district on Prince Edward Island. Although, it sure was going to put a damper on his visit if he couldn't get along with his cousin's only friend.

As Mattie neared the old cow with caution, Winston stayed back to watch her work and give them both space. She spoke to the laboring jersey in a soothing tone, taking care as she assessed the situation. She rolled up her left sleeve and pulled a long, rubber glove all the way up to her arm pit, slathered some lubricant over her arm, then reached into the cow as routinely as any dairy farmer—not necessarily any dairy farmer's daughter.

Despite himself, Winston was impressed. He'd helped his uncle on the farm but was long out of practice. Working in his father's business took all his time the past several years.

After finishing, Mattie walked back toward him, taking care to remove the glove from the inside out. She showed no sign of squeamishness at the slimy residue now tucked within the glove in her hand. He'd have to get back into farm life awhile before he could match her level of composure.

"I can feel the front hooves and the nose. Won't be long. I don't think she's going to need our help delivering, but Joel and the vet are real concerned about milk fever after the calf comes."

"Joel said he'd be coming right after me. And you've brought those calcium supplements. Ol' *Cowsy* is going to be fine." Winston watched for her reaction to his emphasis on the cow's name. Instead of scowling at him this time, he was treated with a half-smile. "You know Samy gave her that name, right? Not me."

"*Nay.*" She shrugged. "But I'll give you the benefit of the doubt."

He laughed, and she responded with a full smile before she walked away to the barn to *redd* up. Maybe she wasn't finding him such a disappointment after all. Strange how much that relieved him.

Or maybe the miracle of new life simply enraptured them both.

CHAPTER TWO

By the time the newborn calf was licked clean by his mother, the baby bull had an audience. Standing outside the fence, Lydia watched alongside Samy and their three-year-old foster son, Owen. Ellen had also joined in the crowd after giving up hope Mattie and Winston were coming back for her at the school.

Mattie kept an eye on both the calf struggling to make his first stand and the reactions of the children. As the calf pushed up on two shaky front legs, Owen's eyes grew round.

Samy turned to her brother. "Don't worry. He can do it."

Tears tickled the back of Mattie's eyes. A few years ago, Samy had come into all their lives as a foster child, barely able to speak. Since Joel and Lydia adopted her, she'd overcome so many challenges related to autism.

The two little ones cheered as the calf's back legs wobbled upright. Owen's face beamed as he looked up to Samy. "Yay, Sissy. He did it!"

Lydia knelt between the two and hugged them to her sides. "We have to be quiet now. We don't want to scare him. Watch. He's going to get his first drink from his *mamm*."

Joel leaned against the fence post, angling himself close to his family on the other side. And Mattie wondered at the perfectness of their family. Lydia hadn't had any children of her own, not yet. And still the four of them were bound by a love as strong as blood.

Why did it seem like God had a perfect plan for everyone, while she felt more like the weak link in His plan? Her childhood taunted her.

Keep up, Mattie.

Why can't you play, Mattie?

Don't bother asking Mattie. She never comes.

Even today, she'd barely delivered the medicine in time. A simple errand that took her twice as long as anyone else and left her exhausted.

"Hey." Winston's voice beside her brought her out of her memories. "There's nothing quite like it, is there?" He nodded at the suckling calf. "*Gott's* creation never ceases to amaze me."

Mattie's reply got stuck in her throat for a moment. "*Ya.* It's a reminder all *Gott* has made is *goot.*" *Gott's* creation did contain so many wonders, yet her thoughts had been questioning His ability when He'd created her.

"I forget that sometimes." He stared down at his feet with the confession.

Really? She looked back to his face and found nothing less than sincerity. "I thought I was the only one."

"Well, now we know there's at least two of us." His brown eyes latched onto hers. He cleared his throat. "Ellen thinks it's too late to go to town now, but I'm happy to give you a ride home. It'll be getting dark, and the buggy will be safe and warm."

"*Danki,* if it's not too much trouble." Her insides swirled around like thick, melted, hot cocoa for the second time since Winston showed up. The man was *goot* for the appetite. A problem with which she didn't need any help.

"No trouble," he answered, then left her in a fast trot toward the barn. She presumed to hitch up the buggy.

Mattie caught Lydia watching her with much the same expression she imagined had been on her own face while watching the children earlier. Then, Ellen gave her a shy smile and stepped closer.

"So, you met my cousin."

"*Ya.* You might have explained your cousin's a man."

"Oh, don't be mad with me." Ellen's happy expression slipped for the first time since Mattie had known her.

"Oh, Ellen, I cannot be angry with you. But don't get your hopes up if you plan on matchmaking."

"Don't you like him?"

"He's nice." And good-looking—an observation best kept unsaid.

"See, the three of us can be friends. That's all that matters, *nay?*"

"You aren't fooling me. But *ya,* we can be friends. Just remember, that's all. I'd hate to see you disappointed." *Or both of us.* "Why don't you ride along? Maybe even stay for supper." *Mamm* wouldn't mind two extras at the table if she got home soon enough to lend a hand. "Mark wouldn't mind, either."

"Now, who's matchmaking, Mattie Beller?"

"Leastwise, she's straightforward about it." Winston came from behind and nudged his cousin with his elbow. He looked straight at Mattie. "Honest and a master at calving."

Ellen's eyebrows raised, and she gave Mattie a triumphant nod.

Mattie bit the inside of her cheek. Ellen was too much, and so was her cousin's praise.

Winston shoved his hands into a pair of gloves and stepped aside. "We better get going, I guess. You, too, Ellen?"

"I wouldn't miss it." Happy with herself, Ellen walked ahead of them.

Mattie let her eyes roll, only to see Winston smiling at her gesture. He leaned closer to her. "She can't help herself. It's in her blood to meddle. Our mothers do the same." His words lilted on a soft laugh.

"So, you're not bothered by being set up . . . with me?" Too late, Mattie wished the last two words back.

"Why not you? We might make very *goot* friends. I'm only here until after Old Christmas in January. It's not long to make a new friend, but I'd like to try."

She had a long list of why-nots, but he ushered her into the covered buggy before she could state them. Ellen slid beside her. When Winston joined from the other side, one reason was clear enough. She was a dairy farmer's daughter with asthma who couldn't shed a single pound—a fact which made sitting this close to an attractive man very uncomfortable.

The mile-long road home had never seemed so far. Even if she could hold her breath for twenty minutes, Mattie was incapable of creating enough space between them to be decent.

She snuck a peek at Winston. He had enough wiggle room to drive and appeared more amused than mortified—admittedly giving Mattie some relief. On the other side, Ellen sat oblivious and almost satisfied. She must really want to see Mark.

"Friends?' Winston's voice was low in her ear, as if they weren't all sardines squished into the same tin can.

"Friends." Mattie offered without an effort to whisper.

Ellen squealed in delight.

Winston set the buggy in motion. "I hear your eyes rolling, Mattie."

Without much room for leverage, Mattie gave her elbow an extra shove toward Winston's ribs.

"Ouch."

Ha! Right on target.

"Just you wait, Mattie Beller. I have almost five weeks to get you back." His playful tone sounded nothing like the teasing she remembered from the boys in her school days.

She nestled back against the seat, less self-conscious of the space she occupied. If anything, he'd eased the tension building up in her body from sitting so uncomfortably.

"Oh, I've handled worse than you. Never fear."

His eyes met hers for a moment before he looked back to the road. As brief as the glance had been, she was almost sure she'd seen a hint of admiration.

Ach, nay. How silly!

As much as she wished he'd found something to admire, she was plainer than plain. He'd discover so himself in less than five weeks. And that would be that.

The atmosphere around the Bellers' family table hummed with conversation as serving utensils and silverware clattered against the dishes piled high with vegetables, braised beef, and whipped potatoes.

Winston was more than pleased when the spot he was offered at the table sat him directly across from Mattie. With a family of nine and two extra guests, he hadn't been sure he'd get an opportunity to know her better during the meal. Watching her interactions with her family had been eye-opening already.

Winston leaned back as a piping hot platter of beef and gravy passed between him and Mattie's twin brother, Mark, to his left.

"Go on. I can see you want a second helping." Mark held the meat dish closer to Winston's plate.

Winston picked up the fork and stabbed another piece. The earthy aroma of the slow-cooked roast proved too hard to resist. Granted, he wasn't putting up much of a fight.

"Catch!" a young voice ordered as a yeast roll hurtled toward him. "You need that to sop up all the gravy."

"Miles. Mind your manners."

"Sorry, *Datt.*"

Herschel Beller sat at the head of the table. His beard and the hair above his ears were white, while the rest of his full head of hair was a dark gray. For most of the meal, he'd remained quiet, much like Mattie, observing the antics of his six sons with an occasional approving nod to show he was listening.

His wife, Maria, chatted eagerly with all her children and her two guests. She expended almost as much energy as the six boys combined, making sure the meal was served to everyone's satisfaction and conversation never lagged. Mattie assisted at every turn, never once having to be asked and never with anything less than a humble gentleness. She anticipated her mother's next move and quietly kept the supper machine running.

He couldn't help imagine that without Mattie, the easy feasting of the Beller family would come to a grinding halt as fast as an unoiled combine could jam up a harvest.

"You gonna eat that or keep staring at my sister?" Another brother, Martin, eyed Winston's plate with an expression dangerously close to criminal.

"You wouldn't steal my dinner, now, would you?"

"Be a sin to waste it."

"Here, I'll give you half." Winston raised his head after cutting off a portion to share with Martin. When he noticed the warm color rising in Mattie's cheeks, he winked to let her know he didn't mind her brother.

"*Danki.*" Martin shoved most of the portion straight into his mouth. "Do you like her?"

Herschel's throat cleared, and Martin slumped down on the bench seat.

Mattie rushed from her seat to collect empty dishes. She dipped her head at his effort to make eye contact. She shouldn't be embarrassed. Winston was amused. Besides, he did like her. Why shouldn't he?

He looked down at the boy. "Of course, I like her." Dishes clattered louder than before. "Jesus says to love everyone, doesn't He?"

Martin's mouth twisted into a frown. "*Ya.* Even girls."

Laughter rippled around the table, but Mattie's back was turned at the sink, where she was unloading an armful of plates. She didn't appear to be laughing. Other than Winston, no one seemed to notice. Except Herschel, who looked back in her direction and ran his fingers through his beard. He turned his attention around to the table again, and his gaze landed right on Winston. Suddenly, Winston forgot what they had all found so amusing.

After a bowlful of tapioca pudding, the younger boys went upstairs to get ready for bed. Ellen stayed in the kitchen to help Mattie and her *mamm* with the clean-up, and Herschel invited Winston to follow him out to the barn.

Walking behind the man, Winston tried to shake off the sense he was in trouble without much success. Winston hadn't been in the community for forty-eight hours yet. The newness of the surroundings and the people were offset to a large degree by their common faith and traditions. Still, he didn't know Hershel. What the man wanted was anyone's guess.

Mattie's *datt* opened the barn door and flipped on a battery-operated lantern.

"Go ahead and grab some feed for Joel's horse. Don't want to send the minister's animal back hungry. I'll get her some water."

Winston exhaled his pent-up breath. "I'm sure he will appreciate your kindness."

"Not so much kindness as a chance to find out more about you." He was as straightforward as his daughter. "I heard you plan to stay all the way through Christmas. What will you do with yourself while you're here?"

"I've only shared this with Joel so far. Of course, I know word will get around once I start looking, but I aim to search for my own land to buy here."

"Problems back home? Trouble with your parents or the bishop?"

"Nothing like that. I was only seventeen when Lydia and Joel got married, but the way Joel talked about this place lit a fire in me that hasn't burned out. My parents and the bishop agreed I needed to spend some time with the Yoders to see if it's just a boyish dream or a yearning from the Lord I need to follow."

"Well, then, I will pray for *Gott's* will to be done."

"That's what I want."

"Now, if you're going to be looking, seriously looking, at land, then my Mattie could be a real help to you. She's the reason I bought this place. Her *mamm* and I were going to offer on a big plot closer to the other families in the New Hope district. This was further than we had hoped. Mattie did some research. Don't ask me what all those papers were she studied and read, but she convinced me this land was better suited to our needs. I've been a dairy farmer since I cut teeth and learned to walk. I know how to make a profit, but this land has raised my production almost double what I ever got in Ontario. Don't you tell her that I told you. She won't like getting any notice. But if you can figure a way to get her interested in your plans, she can steer you in the right direction."

Winston had more to think about than how to get Mattie to agree to help him. Truth was, he wasn't overly comfortable with the idea of having anyone he'd just met that involved in something so personal to him. And an unmarried woman might get the wrong idea—suspect he was entertaining a marriage proposal to go along with the house-shopping.

"Mattie's a nice person and smart. I can see that already, and I'm not too proud to ask for help. I just wouldn't want her feelings getting hurt. But I'll give it some thought."

"Now, I don't want my girl to get hurt, either. If you treat her with respect, there shouldn't be a problem."

Winston hadn't found dealing with women to be so simple, but he knew he could use some help. If Mattie was the Lord's answer to his need, who was he to argue?

He would've liked to know Mattie a little more before involving her in his business. But her own father must know her well enough. And truth be told, she hadn't shown even the slightest interest in him, not in that way.

She'd agreed to be friends. He could keep this businesslike. He was *goot* at business deals. And he wouldn't have to worry about giving her the wrong idea.

Mattie's view from the kitchen window lent a peek at the light coming from the barn and the silhouettes of her father and Winston. *Datt* must have taken some interest in Winston to put off his ritual evening pipe while reading the *Farmer's Almanac* by the woodstove. He was a creature of habit, as *Mamm* liked to say. Maybe Mattie was as well. But then, lately, something was stirring her to more than the routines she wrapped around herself like a blanket of cozy security.

Was it because Ellen had traveled all the way from the States to teach at the New Hope school—a job Mattie had been offered and turned down? She winced. The nagging accusation of cowardice resurged, as it had ever since Ellen arrived.

Mark and Ellen's low voices drifted from the family living room to where she and *Mamm* finished scrubbing and drying the supper pots. At least her fear of change brought about a happy consequence for her brother.

"What has you so deep in thought, Mattie?" *Mamm* handed her a clean skillet to rinse and dry, then plunged a saucepan into the sudsy water, giving it a hard scrub.

"Before you met *Datt*, did you wonder what *Gott* wanted you to do with your life? I mean, what would you have done if you never married?"

The pot clanked as *Mamm* set it down in the sink. She reached for a dishtowel and wiped the soapy water off her hands.

"Well, now, let me think for a moment. That was a lifetime ago." *Mamm* rested a hip against the counter and looked at Mattie in her tender way which told Mattie she had her undivided attention. "I'm not sure I felt as you do. We are so different, you and I. But all young women wrestle with fear of the future, I'm sure, to one degree or another. And you, my sweet *maydel*, have always studied every problem until you are sure of your answer. While most girls blow whichever way the wind tosses them and call it love, you keep your feet planted on solid ground. You've saved your *datt* a great many worries by being so sensible."

Was she being sensible or just facing the truth of the matter? Young women like Ellen had no trouble finding a beau. They could be brave, face change, and explore new possibilities. But the world beyond her parents' farm never met Mattie with favor.

"What if *Gott* made me different because He wants me to stay here with you? Maybe that's all I am made to do."

"*Ach*, Mattie. Let me tell you a secret. *Gott* never shows us His purpose when we are looking inside of ourselves for the answer. It's not there. Only when we look to the needs of others and make ourselves available to serve *Gott* by giving of ourselves can we find meaning in our life. No matter where you live—whether you are single or married—your joy will come from doing whatever thing He has given you to do for that day. As you do His work, He will bring you the desires of your heart."

Mamm handed her the towel and wiggled her eyebrows. "Looks like our work here isn't finished yet."

Mattie accepted the towel. "*Danki, Mamm*."

Mamm's response was to hand Mattie another pot to rinse and dry; then she hummed the tune of a Christmas carol. *God rest ye merry, gentlemen / Let nothing you dismay . . .*

If only Mattie could believe the answer were so simple.

From the kitchen window, Mattie watched her *datt* and Winston walk from the barn toward the house. *Datt* continued around to the front porch, but Winston stopped, held up the lantern so that his face was clear, and motioned her to come.

Was he really asking her to meet him outside?

"Well, Mattie, go on." *Mamm's* gentle push nudged her toward the back door.

She set aside the dishtowel with uncertainty clouding her thoughts. Her mother's raised brow brought a quick end to any consideration of running upstairs to hide in her room instead. Walking outside at night to meet a dangerously handsome man in the dark came frighteningly close to courting. Or at least to her own imaginings and the tales she'd heard. She wouldn't really know firsthand what courting was like, and the fear of appearing foolish slowed her steps.

Winston met her as she rounded the corner of the house. Light from the lantern spilled over to illuminate his broad smile. So, he was happy she came. Relief washed over her, dispersing some of her doubt. How did he continue to manage putting her at ease? And they'd only just met.

"I'll be going, soon as Ellen's ready to leave."

So that was it? He was in too much hurry to come inside to say goodbye. "*Ya*, it was nice to have you come. *Danki* for all you've done for me today."

"Meeting you was a surprise. A *goot* one and unexpected." He lowered his arm and switched the weight of the lantern to the other hand, then eased closer so that both of their faces were visible in the light between them. "Maybe *Gott* knew I needed a helper on my visit here, and His answer is you."

Mattie's heart squeezed with a tremor. Nothing like the pain of shortness of breath from an asthma attack, but paralyzing, nonetheless. In front of her, Winston's confident demeanor slackened. His eyes met hers. Humble. Hopeful.

"I've asked *Gott* to help me with choosing a home for my future." He looked down at his feet for a moment and swallowed before returning his watch to her face. "I asked Him to make two things clear to me on this trip. Is the New Hope district a place where I can join the church and remain committed to the faith? And is there a piece of land where I can build a life to support a family?" He tipped his head close to hers. "That's where you come in."

"Me . . . I do?"

He leaned back at a more comfortable distance. "I need a guide, someone to show me around the area."

"Oh."

"Six weeks isn't very long to make such an important decision, so I can't afford to waste time. You can save me valuable time by helping me focus on the best properties for my needs. Your *datt* says you have a head for maps and numbers. I'm not too proud to admit I haven't. I can make it worth your while. Pay you, even."

"I don't think so."

"All right then, I'll find another way to reimburse you for your effort."

"That's not what I meant. I meant, *nay. Nay* to the whole idea." She couldn't bear to hear another word. "Good night."

Her upbringing didn't allow her to slam the door as she fled to the house. But her heart gave that wooden frame a resounding whack behind her and repeated the same refrain at her bedroom door. She threw herself on to the bed and covered her head with the pillow. She might never exit either door again.

CHAPTER THREE

Winston was well aware of the eyes on him as he entered the home of Abe and Sarah Nafziger for the Sunday church meeting. Not only was he a stranger to most of the congregation, but he'd also arrived with the new minister's family. He imagined they were all curious about his purpose in making such an extended visit to their small community so far from his home, although no one other than Herschel Beller had asked.

No juicy morsels for gossiping tongues lay buried in his past. He hadn't left behind any broken hearts, excluding his *mamm's. Nay,* he was no different than any other ordinary twenty-one-year-old Amish man. The fact he hadn't been baptized yet made him a bit odd, but he fully planned to join the church. He'd never been rebellious against his parents or ever longed for the ways of the outside world. His parents and their bishop couldn't understand his reason for waiting. Mostly, because he couldn't explain what he didn't understand himself.

So, here he was. Nurturing the seed of a dream planted in his mind by Joel Yoder four years ago in hope of an answer. Would he find peace with *Gott* here and join the church at New Hope? Or would he go home, bury the longing to hear from *Gott,* and get on with facing up to his responsibilities where everyone else thought he belonged?

"So? What do you think so far?" Mark Beller fell into step beside him.

"About?"

"Oh, anything, I guess. Life on the island compared to back in Pennsylvania. Or the differences in our church and yours."

Winston wasn't sure he knew enough about either one to make a judgment call.

Mark gave him a shoulder bump. "Or my sister."

"Ya, there's a lot to think about, for sure. I reckon I need more time to tell what I think." More time with Mattie sounded nice; only, he still hadn't figured where he went wrong the other night. He wasn't keen on discussing his failure with her twin either. "The lesson in today's service gave me some food for thought. Joel's preaching was interesting."

"*Ya*, that's what everyone says."

"What about you?"

"Oh, sure. Of course, I agree."

Before this morning, Winston believed he'd heard every sermon there was to be heard, many times over again. Either his wandering mind had missed this one on Jesus' parable of the talents, or Joel had explained this particular Scripture in a new way. He hadn't changed the meaning but made it clearer, in a way that drove the words into Winston's heart.

Mark didn't appear too interested in a discussion on the sermon, more like he was ready to pounce on some lunch and sneak off to wherever he'd been going lately. Did Mattie know her brother drove around in an old sports car most nights? At least, almost every night since Winston arrived.

He and Mark joined a group of young folks waiting for the food to be served, but neither Ellen nor Mattie were to be seen. He'd learned women were very capable of hiding among these gatherings when they didn't want a man's attention. But nary a man could escape a woman if she'd a mind to seek him out. The one thing Mattie had made clear was the fact she was hiding, not seeking. It was more like she wasn't even in the game. Why did that increase his desire to find her all the more?

Winston was supposed to seek *Gott* with all his heart and all his soul, and the time was short for him to decide if that meant joining the Amish on Prince Edward Island. He still hadn't found a better way to go about his search than Hershel Beller's suggestion. He had to try again.

All afternoons were short this time of year. Still, Sundays were the shortest. After helping serve lunch following the worship service, plus a *goot* long visit with all the neighbors, not much daylight remained once the family got back home.

Mattie's favorite thinking spot beckoned her, despite the setting sun. In the opposite direction from the milking barn and near the tree line of the far pasture, an old wooden swing hung from a solid sugar maple many years before her family bought the land. This was the third year she'd passed the seasons under the branches.

The old tree had become something of a dear friend to her—a safe place to calm her fears. She'd rocked gently in the cradle of the swing and gazed upward into the ever-changing foliage as it rustled in the breeze. Its strength held her when she'd swung high in moments of joy, and its faithful presence waited to greet her, come what may. Today, it beckoned her to come and pray, as the best of friends draw one closer to *Gott*.

Winston's presence in church that morning had left her unsettled. Long ago, she'd determined none of the young men in her district were meant for her—not for marriage at any rate. Life had been easier with that decision settled.

That morning, she had been sure Joel's message was another reminder that she needed to be useful with her life. *Gott* gave her talents to profit His work, both now and in His kingdom to come. No matter how few she believed she'd been given, *Gott* would increase them through her faithfulness.

But then, she had been mighty distracted. Her heart kept turning its attention to the new man so apparent on the other side of the aisle. Why had she lost her temper with him? He'd offered friendship, and she'd ruined it. All because for a fleeting moment, she'd hoped he wanted something more.

Her frustration with herself had soured her temper all day and made her cross with her brothers, too. How she needed her tree and a quiet moment to pour out her heart to *Gott*. How she hated to feel this off-balanced. And all because of a man. What was the matter with her?

"Mattie! Wait up."

Mattie turned, unsure who called.

Jogging toward her came the same broad shoulders and wavy hair which had kept her distracted from Joel's sermon that morning. He bent over with his hands on his knees, looking up at her through mischievous brown eyes as he gasped for breath.

In a few seconds, he was standing upright again, fully recovered. If only she caught her breath so fast after a run like that. Why would he run after her, especially after the way she had treated him?

"Is something wrong?"

"*Nay*, your *datt* said I could find you here. But you had a *goot* head start on me."

"*Datt* sent you?"

"*Vass*? Why would he do that?"

"I don't know. That's why I was asking."

"Mattie, I came to see you on my own accord. To ask if you'd like to spend the evening at the Yoders' with me and Ellen. Ellen said you felt a little too old for the singings. And, well, I have to agree I've outgrown the youngies at those events myself. Joel and Lydia offered for us to hang out at their place."

How was she to explain she wasn't up to the trip without embarrassing herself? Without appearing obstinate, again.

"I was going to invite Mark, too, but he's not here."

Of course, he hadn't come just for her. She didn't know if she was relieved or disappointed.

Sometimes, some of the young people would gather at one of the farms and have a hymn sing in the barn. For a while now, she'd outgrown the pastime, but since Ellen came, she'd started to go again. Before Ellen, Mark had rarely attended, either. How curious that he'd decided to go tonight when Ellen wasn't there.

"Come on, Mattie. It will be fun."

The eagerness in his invitation made her heart skip a beat. "*Ya*, I'd like to go, very much. The thing is, I get awful tired out, and I couldn't make that walk tonight."

"You think I'd make you walk? I've brought the buggy. And running after you has me plum wore out, too. We can take all the time you need walking back to your house."

He was thoughtful. She just had to remember not to let it go to her head.

"We did agree to be friends for the next five weeks, *nay*?"

"All right then." She fell into step next to Winston, who shortened his stride considerably compared to his previous jog.

She looked back over her shoulder.

"That might be one of the most beautiful sugar maples I've ever seen." Winston hovered over her.

She tilted her head to see his profile. "I think so, too."

Together, they turned back to make their way across her father's pasture. Perhaps being with real friends was the best thing for her tonight. The swing would be there tomorrow. Besides, she could play a fierce game of Dutch Blitz.

"Hope you don't mind losing to a girl." She fell right into step again.

"Suppose that depends on the girl."

Looking up into his eyes to gauge his meaning turned out to be a mistake. The warmth of his expression weakened a full afternoon's resolve to keep her feelings for him at bay. She could not allow herself to be tricked into thinking he had any romantic ideas toward her.

Even though everyone here was kind to her, unlike the teasing she endured in school, no one had ever gone so far out of the way as to include her. Maybe for Winston, this seemed perfectly ordinary, but her world was floating on a topsy-turvy wave. She only had to remember the embarrassment of her over-imagination the other night to be cured of both giddiness and elation. Winston was a nice person with no idea how much her world lacked handsome Amish men with chivalrous manners. From now on, she'd be polite in return. He deserved at least that much. No more hiding behind closed doors. And if he bothered to ask for her help a second time, she'd take her *mamm's* advice to look to the needs of others above her own.

But she wasn't going to waste one more second thinking of him as anything other than a friend.

CHAPTER FOUR

A five-player game of Dutch Blitz flipped the switch on Mattie's competitive side. More than once in the past few minutes, her hand stole a matching set of cards right out from under Winston's reach.

"I can see I've got to be quick to beat you." Winston grimaced in a mock frown, even as his eyes held the delight of a tease.

Beside her, Lydia laughed and threw down another card. Ellen snatched the card and made a match of her own. If Mark were here to play, there'd be an even six. He was faster than Mattie; and when they teamed up, no one could beat them. Of course, he'd want to team up with Ellen now. So why in the world wasn't he here, anyway?

Too late, she noticed Joel put down a card she needed. Winston wiggled his eyebrows as their hands collided, but he beat her to it. Her face burned with a blush, and Winston's winning smile turned higher still. If he thought he could win by charming her off her game, he'd better think again. She zoned in on the cards in her hand and, in a glance, memorized all the new face-up cards on the table.

"If you can't beat 'em, join 'em." Joel aimed his comment at Winston. "Not the best advice on most occasions, but when it comes to card games with Mattie, you'll find it to be a wise choice."

"I'll keep that in mind."

Mattie's cheeks grew hotter, but not enough to slow her down.

"We don't have teams tonight, cousin, so you're on your own." Ellen gave Winston a jab with her elbow. "I haven't seen Mattie lose yet. She must have given that one to you out of pity."

"*Nay,* I was distracted." The cards stopped moving, and all went silent. What had she said? Oh dear, they thought she was admitting to being distracted by Winston. "What I mean is . . . "

How was she supposed to explain without embarrassing him or incriminating her brother, whose absence had been her concern?

"Mark isn't here. You've never seen a pair like the two of them." Lydia filled in the gap.

Dear Lydia. No wonder Joel had married her almost as soon as he met her. She was a treasure, and now they were all blessed to have her as their minister's wife.

Soon, the cards were exchanging hands again, yet somehow Mattie had lost track of her strategy. She'd never had trouble remembering which cards had been played or where the cards were positioned in front of her for a quick pick when the right match presented itself. So why was she fumbling now?

Winston was the only thing that had changed in her life for a long time, but she wasn't admitting he had anything to do with it. He looked up from the table and caught her watching. His eyes held her transfixed so that her heart pounded and the cards in her hand almost slipped away.

She snapped her focus back to the game. She would not lose, even to the most distracting man on the planet. Not tonight.

Winston enjoyed everything about being with Mattie and hated for the evening to end. After her resounding dismissal of him after supper at her parents' house the other day, he was glad for this second chance with her.

Thankfully, he was her ride home. And he planned to use the extra time well. He opened the buggy door for Mattie and offered a hand to steady her as she stepped inside. Feeling light on his feet, Winston closed the door and walked around to untether Amazon, Joel's beautiful bay mare. If he were at home, he'd take Mattie home in his own buggy. Maybe even his courting buggy. *Ya,* the courting buggy hadn't been used in far too long. He'd clean it up and give Mattie a real ride.

Of course, he couldn't know if she'd even agree to a courtin' ride. So far, she wasn't even willing to ride around with him to look at land. A sweet, slow trip, where she smiled pretty and he leaned a few inches closer in her direction was a definite stretch of the imagination.

Winston steadied himself before opening the driver's side door to the buggy. How had he jumped from a friendly game night to thoughts of courting? When he'd invited Mattie to the Yoders' house earlier, he thought she deserved some fun with folks her own age for a change. He was allowing things to get out of control too fast. He'd better get back to the business of enlisting her help—as a friend.

He reached for the door, determination in his grip.

As he ducked his head into the cab, Mattie turned to face him. She was nervous, or maybe a bit insecure, but so innocent and pure. His head banged against the frame as he shut the door.

"*Ach,* are you all right?"

"*Ya. Ya,* it's nothing," he lied. Sure, his hard skull was fine. The rest of him was not. "But, uh, there's something I wanted to talk to you about."

Mattie's eyes rounded, but then her look changed to concern. "What is it?"

Winston directed the horse in a slow walk to the end of the driveway and stopped at the road. He took a deep breath. Where to start? "I'm not looking for a wife."

Mattie's expression froze, her eyes wider than ever.

He was a *dumkoff*. "What I mean is that I only need a friend. Someone to help me. You're perfect. Perfect, I mean, as a friend and a helper." He really was a bumbling moron. "It's just that you being a woman makes it more complicated."

"It does?"

"*Ya*, sure it does. I don't want to give you the wrong idea. But I enjoy your company, and you're smart. And I want to ask you again for your help. I just don't want to hurt you."

"How would you hurt me?"

"You know, by giving you the wrong idea."

"Nonsense. I don't go around imagining every unmarried man wants me for a wife. If anything, I get accused of being too sensible. Friendship suits me perfectly well. Besides, I'm more than capable of handling hurt feelings here and there."

He'd never intended to fully douse the possibility of more with Mattie, only slow down the sparks he'd felt sure were mutual. Instead, he'd released the quenching tide of friendship, as effective as a high-powered firehose blast to any flickers of romance.

She sounded brave, but he wasn't convinced. Someone had wounded her, and the knowledge stoked an ache deep in his heart. Worse, she could be referring to whatever he'd unwittingly done the other night. He was probably included in the count of those who had offended her

Her *datt* said to let research for the right property be her own idea. How was he supposed to do that? "I could use a guide—someone who knows the area and can help me locate suitable land for my own farm. And someone I can trust to keep my business quiet, for now, until I decide for sure this is what I want to do."

"How big a secret is this?"

"Joel and Lydia know. The only other people I've told on the island are your *datt*—and you."

"Not even Ellen?"

"*Nay.*"

"You trust me that much?"

"I do. I've already seen your *goot* instincts at work. If old Cowsy could trust you enough to help bring her precious calf into the world . . ." He glanced across the seat to see whether she recalled their first meeting as fondly as he did. She narrowed her eyes, but her cheeks were pink, and a grin tickled the corner of her mouth. "I suppose, after all that, I can rely on you to steer me in the right direction around the island."

"I'm sorry about the way I walked off the other night."

"I'll forget it if you will."

"*Danki*, Winston." She straightened her shoulders, then touched her prayer *kapp* with the tip of her fingers in a way he'd noticed several times—especially before she took a decisive sweep to win a round of Dutch Blitz. "I'll do my best to help you."

He believed her and was tempted to squeeze her hand. Instead, he pulled his gaze away from her long, slender fingers resting on the seat beside him. If he'd kept his mouth shut earlier, her hand might be warmly clasped in his own right now. Lesson learned. He flipped the switch for the buggy headlamps.

Joel's drive entered the road right below the crest of the hill. Winston stopped and looked both directions before easing the horse onto the main road.

"Look out!" The sound of Mattie's scream collided with the squeal of burning rubber tires against asphalt. Her hand wrapped firmly around his bicep as he yanked back on the reins. Amazon pranced for a moment, then backed up a few feet until they were safely back in the driveway. Fortunately, they hadn't been all the way in the road; and the car had been in the opposite lane, so Amazon was likely unhurt.

He turned his attention to Mattie, still clinging to his arm. "You okay?"

She blinked and nodded.

"I have to check on the horse and the other driver."

She pressed a hand against her chest and breathed a slow, deep breath. "I can hold Amazon or go get help."

"*Danki*. I'll be right back." He handed her the reins, thankful she was calm in a crisis.

Up close, Amazon appeared to be uninjured. She was as stalwart as Mattie. Across the street, car lights shone at an odd angle from the ditch. Walking closer, he could hear the engine still running. Tires hit the pavement and sprayed gravel from the ditch. Winston jumped back at the realization the driver was taking off. With no more than a few feet to spare from where Winston stood, the black sports car sped away and out of sight.

Shock left him standing in the road longer than was sensible. Winston shook his head and turned back to where he'd left Mattie with the buggy. Only, Joel was leading Amazon toward the barn, and Mattie stood by the curb. She was staring—transfixed—in the direction of the runaway vehicle. Winston didn't need to guess why. He'd seen the driver before. And Mattie would recognize him, even in the low light. On instinct, he reached for her elbow and pulled her closer as the realization dawned.

She fell against Winston's shoulder and cried, "How could he? *Ach, Mark, nay.*"

Winston wrapped his arms around her, as a *goot* friend should do. But he'd never held a friend, or anyone else, so close before. And never had his own heart cracked open so wide at another's tears. He'd hold her a little longer, if only to prevent her from seeing the watery threat stinging his own eyes or his struggle to stem his anger at Mark's carelessness.

Had Joel seen Mark? For sure, Winston wasn't keen on being the one to tell him.

Mattie leaned away from him, and he released his hold of her. Her head hung either from sorrow or embarrassment at the display of emotion. He didn't want the moment to come between them or make their friendship awkward.

Winston lifted her chin so that she looked up at him. "Don't fret overmuch. No real harm has been done."

"Will you tell Joel?"

The minister must not have seen Mark. "Only if you want me to."

"Nay, I cannot bear it."

"All right, but I think you should speak to your brother. He should know he might have hurt you." *And that a real man would have stayed to face the consequences of his actions.* He didn't expect Mattie to say so to her brother, but Winston had a good mind to do so himself.

"*Danki,* Winston."

The thanks lost its sweetness as it settled alongside a nagging sensation this agreement was the result of poor judgment on his part. He'd wanted to console the pretty girl who had fallen in his arms for comfort. But secrets and cowards made very close kin. And he may be guilty of a similar fault to the one he'd found in Mattie's brother.

He didn't know what kind of minister Joel Yoder would be in these circumstances, although he did know Bishop Nafziger had a reputation for being lenient and kind. "Don't you think Joel deserves to know?"

"*Ya* . . . it's just that *Mamm* and *Datt* will be brokenhearted. They moved here to take us away from the bad influences and friends my brother had begun to follow. Maybe I can talk to him. Maybe . . ."

"Maybe Joel could help him." Winston wasn't one to run to the minister with every misdeed, but Joel's horse and a near miss at the edge of his own driveway made the matter Joel's business if he wanted to know. Besides, in his conversations with Joel, Winston found him both helpful and wise.

"I'm not asking you to lie. If Joel asks, then you must be truthful. I just want to give Mark one more chance. Please, let me talk to him first and see."

"Well, then, I'll pray for *Gott's* will. For now, let's see how we can get you home."

CHAPTER FIVE

Mattie's sleep, what paltry amount she was granted, had been hard won through the night. Her brother's image woke her continually. Grasping through the dark, she found the clock on her nightstand. Bringing it closer, the phosphorescent hands marked the time at three-thirty. Glad for once she had no sister to share her room, she lit the gas lamp, rather than dress in the dark, and wondered when Mark had finally come home.

Tiptoeing past her brothers' rooms, she crept out to the barn to clear her head before milking time. Outside, the spot reserved for the courting buggy remained vacant, and the faint clop of hooves sounded down the lane. She'd be talking to Mark sooner than expected.

Still angry, she couldn't help but relish the idea of a surprise ambush. Did he know he'd almost t-boned his own sister with his reckless driving? And to be such a coward as to leave without a word of apology or sign of concern. She could still go to the barn to sort through her feelings and find a measure of forgiveness before approaching her brother. But then, when would she have such a private opportunity again?

The cold nipped at her nose and the tips of her ears, exposed from leaving the house without her scarf. She cupped her hands and blew into them to warm her face. Mark would be half-frozen from exposure in the courting buggy. Although, he hadn't traveled too far. Winston had shown her the dilapidated shed, where he kept the horse and buggy hidden while he cruised around in his sports car. How many other secrets did her brother keep? Vacillating between feelings of betrayal and pure idiocy for being so naïve, she was still unsure how to approach him.

She marched toward the barn and her brother unhitching the poor creature who had waited on him all night. In less than one week, Winston had noticed more than Mattie ever knew about her brother's habits. Did everyone know except for her, *Mamm*, and *Datt*?

"Mattie? What in the world are you doing?" Mark met her, leading the horse beside him. He thrust the barn door open.

Up close, he appeared annoyingly innocent. By the lantern light, his eyes reflected genuine concern. Rather than the forgiving spirit she'd prayed for, Mattie's anger flared. "Don't do that."

"Do what? Get you out of the cold?" Taking her arm, he pulled her into the warmth of the barn and pushed the doors closed behind them. "What's going on?"

"Don't act like nothing has changed—like I don't know—as if I'm too dumb to know anything."

"Listen, Mattie." His patience sounded as thin as the veil holding back the torrent of her tears. "You have to tell me what this is about. I'm not a mind-reader."

She wouldn't cry. Tears would gain his sympathy, but she wanted his respect.

You could have killed me.

Nay, he'd accuse her of being hysterical. Where was she supposed to begin with him looking at her in earnest concern?

"Why did you drive away?"

He stilled.

"Around dark, you almost ran into me in Joel Yoder's buggy. Your car ran into the ditch, and then you drove away without checking to see if anyone was hurt. Winston was going to see if you needed help, but you nearly ran him over in your hurry to get away. I don't understand, Mark. Why?"

Fear, more like horror too real to be an act, reflected in her brother's eyes. "Mattie, I didn't see you. Or Winston." He drew his hand over his eyes and dropped onto a bale of straw. "You have to believe me. I dropped my phone. When I reached for it, I accidentally swerved into the wrong lane. I over-corrected and went into the ditch. I never saw you, but I did see Joel coming out of his house. That's when I took off. Honestly, sister, I didn't know anyone else was around."

Ach, the relief. All night, she'd wrestled to reconcile the brother she loved with the actions she'd witnessed. "I believe you."

"But that doesn't make things right. Was anyone hurt?"

"*Nay*. Thank *Gott*. Joel's mare was skittish afterward but not injured. Winston hitched up one of the draft horses to bring me home."

"I'll apologize to Joel before I leave."

"Leave for where? Where have you been spending all your time? Obviously not with Ellen, like I imagined."

"Don't get your hopes up about anything between me and Ellen. I enjoy talking to her is all, but I won't marry an American." He was too defensive. And since when did he have a thing against Americans? "Now, you on the other hand might be interested in a certain American visitor."

"Don't tease me, Mark. I've hardly slept all night from worry. You can at least give me some honest answers."

He rubbed a piece of straw between his palms, so the end spun like the top of a merry-go-round. Exhaling a slow breath, he dropped the straw and pushed off the bale to stand beside her. "I can tell you, for sure, I won't be settling down for a long while yet."

"Why is that?"

He leaned closer, his voice low, and his expression serious. "I'm going back to Ontario. And seriously, Mattie, keep it quiet for now. I planned to tell *Datt* first, just haven't worked out how."

Mattie stepped back, suddenly conscious there was more at stake in this business than hiding a sports car and staying out late at night.

"Why Ontario? I thought you left those old ways behind you." For sure, she didn't smell alcohol on him, another reason she believed his version of events. But his explanation offered precious little to ease her mind.

"This isn't the same. I was young and foolish. *Datt* was right to take me away from some of those influences."

Some? Not all. Which ones?

"I have a job lined up for the new year. Everything is all planned. I only ask you to give me more time—before everything changes for good."

"I don't understand what's so hard to tell *Datt*. He will understand if you choose to make a living in the old community."

He winced, and she recognized the stubborn set of his jaw. He was holding back. He was going to walk away and leave her with more unanswered questions than when they began.

"You're a grown man now. Talk to *Datt* and be done with this hiding and prowling around at all hours." She lured him back with the challenge to his manliness.

He took the bait, spinning back to face her with a ferocity she hadn't expected.

"And you're a woman, Mattie. How long are you going to hide behind *Mamm's* skirts? I know you better than anyone, and I know you have the potential to do more with your life. Instead, you hide your talent and use your health as an excuse to do nothing."

"That's not fair."

"Someone has to tell you the truth."

"Says the one with all the secrets."

"You're right. And I will explain everything. I just want to let *Mamm* have this last Christmas."

"You're leaving . . . " Mattie sucked in a deep breath. " . . . leaving the Amish."

"Mattie." His voice resonated deep with warning. "Not now."

Her head ached with the strain to understand. How had she failed to see this coming?

The barn door opened, and her *datt's* face glowed in the light of his upheld flashlight. "What are you two doing out here?" His light flickered behind him as he swung his arm in a backward motion. "*Kumm*, son. Time to get the cows in for milking."

Mark stood, giving Mattie a warning glance before heading outside with their *datt*. His eyes were heavy. She still didn't know where he had been all night, but she nodded a silent agreement to remain quiet for now.

Datt looked over his shoulder to Mattie. "Be a *goot* daughter and fetch the eggs. Your *mamm* wasn't feeling too well last night."

"*Ya, Datt.* I'll take care of it." Just as she'd be the one to mend their mother's shattered heart unless Mark changed his mind.

CHAPTER SIX

As Mattie held her peace and worked alongside her *mamm* to finish the mountain of laundry created by a family of nine, she found one comfort, sad though it was. If Mark followed through with his determined course, at least he would never have joined the church and would not be shunned.

Ach, but her heart stung sore from his accusations against her. Apparently, he felt himself brave and bold in his shocking actions, whereas Mattie was weak and cowardly in her comfort close to home. She'd debated the same in her own private thoughts, but to hear her own brother speak such was unbearable.

The inglorious, never-ending, and most unromantic lines of clothing, which hung on racks to dry in the warm living room, began to blur. *Nay*, she pinched two fingers against the bridge of her nose to stay the rising tears. A coward she may be, but she wasn't going to give another inch to self-pity or gloom. It was time to set aside thoughts of her brother. He would choose his own way, and she would choose hers.

Gott, help me to choose right.

The bang of the kitchen door startled her. Was it lunch time already?

"Mattie! You have a phone call." Myles' voice, still wavering between childhood and early youth, called to her.

"There's a boy on the phone for Mattie. There's a boy on the phone for Mattie." Either Micah or Mason chanted in the other room. Maybe both of them, reminding Mattie of the joys of being a twin when she was young. Of having someone to share in everything.

"Go on!" she motioned the three boys out the door, as she grabbed her coat from a peg. "I'm coming."

Myles walked with her as far as the barn. "I offered to take a message, but Winston insisted on talking to you himself." Her brother shrugged and headed off to return to his work.

Funny thing, she'd assumed all along the caller was Winston, even though Myles never said so. Her stomach was aflutter. The morning's previous gloom vanished.

Mason and Micah nipped at her heels down the lane to the phone shed. She stopped and pointed a finger, first at one and then the other. "Don't you have chores to finish?"

"We're done." These two were most always in perfect unison.

"Ya, well, you can't be following me. Or maybe you'd like to go fold some laundry."

Together, they ran in the opposite direction, singing as they went, "Mattie has a boyfriend. Mattie has a boyfriend."

Years ago, she'd have been mortified. Today, the little ones' antics tickled her. What a mess and a handful those two were. On a normal Monday, they'd be pestering their school teacher, but this one was a teacher workday.

As she reached the shed to answer the phone, a snowflake fluttered down toward her face and landed on her lashes. Face lifted heavenward, a flurry of large flakes swirled high above her and slowly settled toward the earth, landing on her *kapp*, then her shoulders, and finally her one outstretched hand.

By the look of it, soon all would be white with snow. Winter's cleansing. With the thought, a newfound peace settled in her spirit. Mattie stepped into the shelter and picked up the phone.

"Hello, Winston."

The call had been a somewhat hasty decision. Winston tapped his father's business cell phone against his chin and relished the outcome of the call before returning the device to his trouser pocket.

He scribbled the Bellers' road number onto the back of a pamphlet he'd picked up in town and handed it to the cab driver. "I'll be stopping here instead."

The man read the address. "I know the place. Dairy farm, right? No problem."

"I appreciate that." Winston settled back in his seat.

When he'd left the Bellers' home the night before, there'd still been no sign of Mattie's brother. Truth was, he'd been anxious about Mattie ever since. By the time he'd finished his business in town, he couldn't wait to check on her any longer. He'd used the excuse of asking her to come with him when he returned to Montague tomorrow. He surely hadn't anticipated an invitation to lunch, but had accepted with pleasure.

The weather outside his window drew his attention back to the present. "First snow of the year?"

"Yup. 'Bout time, too. They say we could get a foot or more. Me and the wife paid a pretty penny for trail passes this year and haven't got to use them yet."

"Trail passes?"

"Snowmobiling on the Confederation Trail—runs along the old rail line across the island. You gotta pay for a season pass, but snowmobilers get access to the trail during winter. The wardens keep it in tip-top shape around here. Good, clean, family fun—you know what I mean?"

"I've never ridden a snowmobile, but friends in Montana took me cross-country skiing. Might not be the same, but it was a wholesome experience, like you said."

"Yeah, that's cool. You should try trailing on a snowmobile. I bet you'd like it."

Winston wasn't going to explain how un-Amish snowmobiles were considered by the church. "I appreciate that idea. Thanks."

This trip was informative, if not exactly what he'd hoped for. There wasn't much by way of land for sale. The realtor suggested spring as a better time to shop for property. In the meantime, he'd notify Winston if more became available. He had to trust *Gott's* timing in the matter. What could he do about it, anyway?

After the let-down at the realtor's office, he'd scoured the library and visitor center and discovered plenty of local interest activities to keep him and Mattie busy for weeks. In some ways, he was relieved there was no longer a reason to convince her to study land maps for his plans to begin a maple farm—not until more property hit the market.

Instead, he'd have her join him in the interest of getting to know the way of life on the island. All he really intended was to get to know his guide. A fact he'd keep to himself.

His taxi pulled to the edge of the Bellers' lane. He paid the driver and made his way toward the house. A dusting of white already covered the ground.

He neared the house and saw Mark waiting by the front steps.

"Can we speak for a moment?" Mark gestured toward a pair of chairs on the far end of the covered porch.

Winston sat and took his first long look at Mattie's twin. He imagined the curls locked away under his sister's *kapp* and wondered if they matched her brother's unruly ones, which topped his head with the identical mix of light brown colors. Mark's eyes were hazel, though. And where Mattie was soft with curves, Mark was hard with muscle. The two struck Winston as different as night from day. Mattie being the sunshine of the pair.

Mark took the chair in front of him and cleared his throat. "I won't keep you in the cold long. Mattie told me what happened last night."

"Seems to me you were there."

"I was, but I didn't see you. Or Mattie." As Mattie's brother explained his version of the events, Winston considered the odd angle of the car in the ditch and figured the man was telling the truth. Mark continued, "I apologize. And I'll be talking to Joel about it soon, too."

"I accept your apology." Winston leaned forward to stand.

Mark held up a hand to pause him. "I asked Mattie to keep what she knows quiet for now. Just until closer to the end of the year, after Christmas, for our *mamm's* sake."

Without warning, the feel of Mattie in his arms and her anguished cry for her brother returned forcefully to his conscious. He felt an innate need to protect her from the pain her brother's choices were bound to bring. Still, Mark was her twin, and she loved him deeply.

"It's your story to tell." Winston knew his reply came out curt, almost a challenge. He didn't appreciate being put under obligation to this man, who so far had proven reckless, no matter the excuse. He stood, ready to be done with the matter. "Unless you give me reason to do otherwise, I'll keep it that way."

Mark offered no reply, and no footsteps followed behind Winston as he walked across the porch.

At the door, Mattie's face appeared behind the screen. Her warm smile assured she hadn't heard any of his conversation with her brother and was a beautiful reminder of why he'd come.

"You're just in time." She opened the door. "Lunch is ready."

"Shoo, Mattie." Water and soap bubbles from the lunch dishes flew off *Mamm's* fingertips as she waved them. "Get yourself out of this kitchen and in there with the man who has no business being here this afternoon, aside from a desire to be with you."

"Not so loud," Mattie whispered in an effort to make her mother do the same. Then, "Do you really think so?"

"Ach, daughter, believe me. Now, go."

Mattie wouldn't argue but doubted very much the urgency was necessary. Outdoors was a practical whiteout. Winston couldn't leave, even though he may very well wish to do so. Still, the words planted the smallest seed of hope. Was he really here because he wanted to be with her?

She couldn't fathom what had possessed her to ask him for lunch— or for him to invite her to town with him tomorrow, for that matter. Now, no one may be going anywhere for a day or more, except by sleigh or snowmobile. She didn't want to contemplate that disappointing thought either.

She hesitated in the doorway to the living room. Mark, with his feet propped on a stool and a scowl darkening his face, caught her eye first. Then a peal of laughter drew her attention to the rug in the middle of the room, where her two youngest siblings lay in a pile on top of their visitor. Half-grown Myles and Michael sat on the floor a few feet distant, looking too old to join but enjoying the mayhem, nonetheless.

"*Kumm,* daughter." *Datt* motioned to the seat next to him. "May as well enjoy the frolic, as little else can be done until this storm passes."

"Or the cows bellow to be milked." She plopped down next to her father.

"Or that." *Datt* sighed.

A roar ripped through the air, and Mattie jumped. Micah and Mason's hoots of glee came next as Winston sat upright. The twins fell to the floor on either side of him. Just then, his arm shot out to steady a drying rack full of clothes before the whole lot tumbled to the floor.

Mattie covered her heart with her hand. "*Danki.*"

Before Winston had a chance to reply, the twins were yanking on his arms again. "Please, be the bear again."

"Let the man have some peace," *Datt* instructed the boys, who hung their heads but obeyed.

"A bear?" Mattie feigned confusion.

Winston responded with a wink as he pushed off the floor and came to sit in the narrow opening on the sofa between her and her father.

Datt growled low under his breath, no bear imitation intended, then raked his fingers through his beard.

Winston showed no sign of remorse, but Mattie felt the burn of a blush all the way to the tips of her ears.

The scrape of the stool underneath Mark's feet punctuated the silence as he pushed it forward and stood. As he passed the twins, he mussed their hair, then disappeared upstairs. Likely, he hadn't slept yet. He had a few short hours before milking time.

Datt moved to the chair Mark abandoned. Before long, his chin dipped, and his beard bobbed against his chest. He never was able to sit still long without drifting off to sleep.

Out the window behind him, the snow continued. Mattie could see across the yard to the pines weighed down with the weight of accumulated snow bowing the branches.

"Boys, get on your coats and boots. We'll go play . . . " There was no need to finish, as they whooped in excitement and ran for the back door. Winston watched them go, then shifted his attention to her, expectant. "Want to come?" she offered.

"Only if you're going." His left cheek dimpled. The first she'd seen it. Her heart flip-flopped in response.

Outside, the temperature hung right at the freeze point and created a wet snow, mostly useful to the boys for stomping into a muddy mess. Still, they were happy, and the energy they burned outdoors was better than indoors, making a mess of her clean laundry and the men grouchy for lack of a nap.

A blanket of snow covered everything else in sight. It lay like a patchwork quilt atop a ripple of hills with the color of pine needles stitched in green through white of purest cotton.

Winston's arm brushed against her shoulder. He was so tall beside her, while truly only a bit above average height. His gloved hand squeezed her mittened one. The contact was short but laden with meaning. To her at least. No man had ever held her hand before.

She wondered if Winston had ever held another in the way he comforted her as she cried over her brother. He'd been so gentle and kind. Not for even a moment had he made her uncomfortable or caused her regret for exposing her feelings so openly.

Would he take her hand again—longer?

"This land is beautiful." He wasn't looking at the wintery expanse. He was looking at her.

"It has made a *goot* home for us." *And would for him, also,* she didn't dare to say aloud.

Around them, a sudden quietness settled. The boys must have grown cold and returned to the house. She had no desire to follow.

Winston moved in front of her. Dark splotches on his coat revealed the dampness of both snow and air. His honey-colored hair curled around his ear and clung to his hat, also wet with beads of melted drop- lets. His eyes met hers and lingered until she felt very warm, despite the falling snow. "I'm discovering all I wished for and a fair bit more."

Suddenly, she thought he might kiss her. Instead, he tapped a finger on the tip of her nose and turned his head to gaze up the hill.

"I should go. Joel may need help, and it's no short walk."

She wanted to plead with him to stay, but vows of friendship held her back. "I'm sorry you'll have to walk in such a storm."

He looked back down on her. The dimple returned. "Don't be. It will be worth every step with you in my memory."

She remained in the spot where he'd left her until he disappeared from view altogether. He'd come for her tomorrow, he'd said. Maybe by then, she'd remember she was only a friend to him—and convince herself she felt the same.

CHAPTER SEVEN

Winston had come close to ruining any chance he had a of long-lasting relationship with Mattie. He'd almost kissed her friendship and any possibility of more goodbye. A misstep he'd been kicking himself over for two days.

He fanned the fire in the schoolhouse's potbelly stove. Ellen would arrive soon, ahead of her students, and he still didn't have the room warm for her. He didn't envy her being cooped up in this place with more than twenty youngsters who'd missed the past two days of school. Almost two feet of snow had fallen the other day and delayed his trip to town with Mattie as well.

Winston had learned that snow was not the same everywhere. The land and the reaction of the people varied vastly from place to place. His visit to Montana taught him to enjoy a good snowfall for all it was worth. He hadn't enjoyed playing in the snow since he was a boy, until that trip. The experience of biking up the mountain trails, then hiking to find the perfect slope, followed by the thrill of the downhill and cross-country skiing was one of his fondest memories.

And that cab driver had given him the perfect way to share the same joy with Mattie.

Apparently, anything was possible with enough money. While he wasn't in danger of running out, this little adventure was going to cost him a pretty sum. His *mamm* would accuse him of all sorts of worldliness if she knew the amount. But this experience for Mattie was worth the price.

He shivered and looked up to the school entrance. A cold gust had come in with his cousin. Ellen shut the door as fast as she'd opened it.

"Might not want to remove your coat yet. It's still chilly in here." Winston hoped she heard his unspoken apology.

She came closer and warmed her hands over the stove.

He hadn't mentioned his plans to Joel. In this case, he figured asking forgiveness might be the better route than seeking permission. Wouldn't hurt to get Ellen's opinion, though, so he explained his whole idea to her.

Ellen shook her head at him. "I don't know. You're taking a big risk. I don't think Mattie has ever done anything quite so . . . "

"Adventurous," he offered. "That's just it. I want to give her a new experience."

"I was going to say wild, or fast, or . . . un-Amish."

"Exhilarating. I think that's the word you're looking for, right, Teacher?"

His cousin wrinkled her nose at his teasing.

"I suppose you remember how I met Mattie. Delivering that new calf was exhilarating, and Mattie was a natural. She has more gumption than others seem to recognize."

"That's not the same, and you know it."

True, but he wasn't about to fully explain his reasoning to Ellen. Holding Mattie's hand. Almost kissing her. Winston was sure both were a bigger thrill than anything he had planned for their outing today.

"Go ahead then. I can tell your mind is made up. Don't say I didn't warn you when she refuses."

"I wish you could come, too. We could go a different time." He didn't want to wait, but he should include his cousin. "Maybe Mark would come."

"*Danki*, but I don't think that's a wise idea."

"You don't want to see Mark, then."

"*Nay*. I'd rather not."

Winston was glad to hear it. Ellen's heart was sure to get crushed if she set it in his direction.

"When you get back, there's something I'd like to talk to you about."

"Has something happened at home?" He knew she'd received mail from her sister in yesterday's post.

"There's no bad news from home, and this can wait. Go have a *goot* time. I shouldn't have mentioned it." She waved him off. "Tell Mattie hello for me."

He pushed away the worry something more was the matter than Ellen was saying. She'd been rather solemn since Sunday. But then, the women in his family could be moody. Maybe she was just in one of those womanly times. Ellen would tell him her troubles in time.

Outside, he called the driver he'd arranged for before the children began to arrive. Dan King was the Yoders' neighbor and friend, an older gentleman whom they trusted, and more affordable than a cab.

Winston's excitement was building by the minute. Mattie deserved some fun. She quietly served her parents, a passel of siblings, and her Amish community whenever they called. Her asthma and shyness kept her confined. More than anything today, he longed for her to enjoy a taste of freedom. Freedom to be herself—with him.

Mr. King arrived in his silver minivan. They passed the four younger Beller boys walking to school and soon arrived at Mattie's home. She was waiting on the porch when they arrived. Dressed warmly, as he'd warned her to do. Her movement was a little stiff in the long, down coat and high snow boots.

He opened the van door and helped her up into the seat behind the driver. Hurrying around to the other side, he climbed into the seat beside her and shut the door.

She tugged at her mittens until both hands were free. Her cheeks were rose red, and she fanned herself with a mitten. "Goodness. I'm likely to have a heat stroke so bundled up." She shot an accusing glance his way. "You really think all this is necessary?"

If he explained too much, she may tell him to take her right back home. "You'll be glad when we get there."

She raised an eyebrow. "Get where?"

"Dan is going to take us to Cardigan, where we'll meet a guide who's going to take us on a tour."

"A tour of Cardigan?"

"Not the places you've seen. We'll get a beautiful view of the country; and with all the snow the storm brought, it's going to be incredible." His conscience burned from the manipulative deception.

She bit her lower lip and looked away from him out her window.

"Mattie, you won't have to walk or hike. I'll look out for you, I promise. I've arranged everything, so you can enjoy *Gott's* creation. And we will do all of it together."

She looked down at her hands, clasped together in her lap. "I'll hold you up. Be in your way. You should have asked me first. I'd have told you so."

"*Nay*, you won't." With everything in him, he wanted to reach over and take her hand to ease her fear, but he sensed Dan watching his every move. "This trip is for you. I want you to have fun. I'll take care of you." He twisted sideways in his seat and bent closer to her. "Please, Mattie, give it a chance?"

"I'll try." Her posture remained non-committal, but her shoulders relaxed as some of the tension released.

Maybe Ellen was right, and this adventure was doomed before it began. It had seemed perfect when the plans had come together so well. He'd called the cab company and spoken with the driver again. The fellow knew a guide who'd rent a machine and take a beginner on a run over the area around the outskirts of Cardigan. The warden of the island's eastern trail assured him the snowmobile groomer would be out preparing the trail that night. All Winston had to do was contact the guide to arrange the details.

But how did he explain it all to Mattie?

"Have you ever been to Montana?" Winston could almost see her worried thoughts dissipate as curiosity replaced them.

"*Nay.* Why do you ask?"

"I visited some Amish there a couple years ago." He didn't want to explain how successful his *datt's* business had been, allowing him to travel all over the U.S. to different Amish communities. Not only would he sound boastful, but he also had a different point. "They took me skiing. I had to learn how, first, and then we went down the mountainside. I've never felt so close to *Gott* in all my life, as I did in that experience. I felt His power and His nearness in a way I'll never forget."

The color in her face disappeared. "I cannot ski, Winston."

He did take her hand now. It was cold to his touch. He held it tight, pleading for her attention. "I'm not taking you skiing."

"Even if you tried, I wouldn't go." She snatched her hand out of his. Color returned to her cheeks, though not as scarlet as before. He loved her spirit and the challenge of it.

"How about a snowmobile ride?" His conscience eased, if only a fraction, at the confession of his plan. Snowmobile riding while on holiday would probably be overlooked by his bishop. Or at least, there was some chance it might be, since the rules relaxed considerably during vacation trips.

But Mattie wasn't on vacation.

Her sharply raised brow pushed him to continue before she could turn him down. "What I want to do for you is try to recapture that feeling of being close to *Gott* while surrounded by His creation. I know you milk cows and gather eggs, plant and sow in a garden, and watch glorious snowfalls in your own backyard. But I'd like to show you nature from a different point of view. One that I hope you will treasure as well."

Winston held his breath and waited. And waited. He should tell Dan to turn the van around.

"That sounds like a gift. A very special one."

Her soft voice restored his breathing, and he soaked in her meaning before responding.

"*Ya*, I suppose it is an early Christmas gift, from me to you."

"I won't deny, I am feeling a little frightened, but I am also pleased. *Danki*, for being so kind." She briefly laid her hand on top of his. The momentary touch, the first one of her own accord, set his heart to pounding.

Did she have any idea how far his heart had progressed beyond anything remotely close to the truce of friendship they'd struck? He knew she didn't. And he had no idea how to go from here.

Trees and snow melded into a blur as Mattie clung to Winston atop the speeding snowmobile. Once her initial fear subsided, she'd been able to peer around his shoulder to watch the scenery flash by them at an alarming rate.

Her legs stung with cold, despite the thick leggings under her skirt. At least, Winston's body shielded most of hers from the biting wind as he drove. She focused on leaning right or left with him to keep their balance. If the guide ahead of them was taking this slow for their sake, how fast would he go alone? She wanted to squeeze Winston's shoulder to signal she'd like to slow down but didn't dare loosen her grip around his waist. For some reason, Winston believed she would enjoy this. After all the effort he'd taken to make the arrangements, she didn't have the heart to let him down by refusing to ride. *Ach,* but *Datt* would disapprove.

If Winston had asked her first . . .

Her fists clutched his thick parka, ears ringing with the roar of the engine, eyes wide open to absorb the vastness of the snowy countryside, and the rhythm of her body swaying back and forth in tandem with the natural curve of the land.

Over the snow-covered railbed they sped, along the path thousands of passengers had taken across the Maritimes in a time long gone. Lives all but forgotten, yet alive to her in this moment they shared.

She'd never experienced the power of *Gott's* creation to the filling of all her senses as she was this moment. The Father's nearness enveloped her. Then the trees fled into the backdrop, and the ground spread wide in front of them to make way for the ocean beyond.

For a moment, she thought they may stop. Instead, they made a sharp left and followed the trail along the cliffs and downhill toward the beach. Waves crashed against the rocks far below them, the spray as white as the snow on which they were gliding. All of the sudden, she was struck by the magnitude of the loss had she chosen not to come. This once, she'd thank Winston for not asking ahead of time.

The drivers slowed again, perhaps reined in by the same awe she felt. The trail continued to weave near the shoreline, sometimes further inland to remain on the path with enough snow, but always returning to a view of the shining sea stretched forever to their east.

Facing the same direction, she rested against the incline of Winston's back. Her head was heavy from the weight of her helmet, and her arms were weak from maintaining such a tight grip. She relaxed, watching and waiting for glimpses of the water coming like the melody of a song interspersed with the harmony of the woods woven between the highs and the lows.

This was worship—encompassing peace, reverence, and nearness with the Almighty of Heaven and Earth. Her spirit burst into song, though her lips could not.

The Lord is *my light and my salvation; whom shall I fear?*[1] The psalmist's question from her morning Scripture reading floated on the tune welling in her heart. She'd spent too many years in fear of almost everything. No more. The Lord of all of this, the One who held her very soul in safety, He was her strength. Whatever He asked of her, she would no longer be afraid.

The snowmobile slowed to a full stop. Their guide walked toward them. Winston removed his helmet, but Mattie opted to flip up the visor instead. Whenever she removed the tight-fitting contraption, her hair and prayer *kapp* were sure to be in shambles.

---

1 Psalm 27:1

"We'll turn inland now, toward the golf course and the restaurant. Thought you may like a minute to enjoy the scenery. And I just wanted to check and make sure you're doing fine behind me."

"Sure." Winston tugged off his gloves and ran his fingers through his hair, away from his forehead. He managed to bring his leg over the seat to stand beside the machine without kicking Mattie behind him. He held out a hand to her and eased her onto her own two feet. He turned his attention back to the guide. "This is a nice piece of machinery. I didn't have a bit of trouble. It was a nice, smooth ride." Winston looked at her. "What did you think, Mattie?"

"It was faster than I imagined." She wouldn't say *no* trouble, when she knew there was plenty ahead when her *datt* found out.

The guide smiled. "That's a compliment. Snowmobiles can be finicky to keep running smooth, and speed is the object. I'm glad you've enjoyed your ride so far. Feel free to walk down into the cove if you'd like. You might even find a shell to keep as a souvenir." He pointed at a narrow path leading toward the shore. "Next stop is the best little diner on the east shore for a hot meal after a long ride."

As glorious as the ride had been, Mattie couldn't bring herself to trudge along the beach looking for shells in so much uncomfortable clothing. She'd rather finish sightseeing on the snowmobile. Then, she'd find a washroom and try to return her clothes and hair into some semblance of respectability before they re-entered the world.

"I think I'm ready for that meal," Mattie hinted to Winston in Pennsylvania German.

"All right, then. We can go." He nodded, but disappointment crossed his features. "I'll tell him." Only the guide had already walked away. "Are you sure you don't want to spend just a few minutes along the beach? I had hoped . . . " His words were lost to her in his unspoken thoughts, but his eyes remained fixed on hers. Gentle. Hopeful.

Her heart skipped a beat.

He might kiss her, alone by the shore, but of course, he couldn't. The enormous safety helmet which made her look like a fat-headed alien dispelled all romantic ideas.

"I can help you take off the headgear, if it's bothering you." Was he reading her mind already?

"*Nay!*" No matter how his caramel eyes and kindness softened her into a compliant puddle, she'd uncover her hair for one man alone—her husband. For sure, a husband who gave gifts like this one today would be awfully nice.

Winston, of course, wasn't thinking any such thoughts. He'd imagine her prayer *kapp* and hair all still neatly arranged underneath the awful contraption. As if removing it would be no different than for a man.

"We can go seashell hunting another time. I have a favorite beach. I'll take you there."

"That's an offer I'll make sure to redeem, Mattie."

Would he?

Somehow, she sensed she'd made a terrible mistake, ruining a beautiful might-have-been for the both of them. All because she was afraid to remove a helmet. Or maybe what terrified her the most was the idea of her first kiss.

How had things with Winston changed so fast? Once again, she just couldn't keep up.

Winston had been sure Mattie was enjoying the ride as much as he'd hoped. And then, she'd gotten skittish, like a customer almost sold on a product until the salesman became too aggressive. He'd seen the look many times in his father's business. And he'd become his *datt's* righthand man because he never pushed a client so far. For the life of him, he couldn't figure how he'd bungled the outing with Mattie.

He looked up from the table in the crowded, local restaurant dining room. Mattie had excused herself to the washroom, and he wanted to make sure she saw where they'd been seated when she came out. He waved at her as she rounded the corner from the front of the building. She saw him and headed in his direction. Only a few people stopped to stare. He knew they were intrigued by her Amish clothing and head covering. He, on the other hand, was simply captivated by the sweetness of her presence.

She wasn't some client or potential customer to him. And he was no longer willing to see her as only a friend. Maybe that was why he struggled. Work came easy for him. But whatever was happening in his heart regarding Mattie Beller had him in a rare state of wordless wonder. How had he come to fall head over heels with this woman in such a short time?

He couldn't account for it. There didn't seem to be any way of stopping it, and he no longer had any desire to try. He just hadn't figured out the right way to proceed.

"Did I take too long?" She scooted up to the table in the chair across from him.

"*Nay*, I ordered you a hot chocolate and a water to drink. I hope that's okay."

"Of course, *danki*. A hot drink sounds perfect about right now." She picked up the menu as the waitress returned with their drinks.

"I think you are our first Amish customers. Locals love our place, but we're kind of hidden off the beaten path. Glad you found us." The woman smiled as she retrieved a pen and notepad from her apron pocket. "Need any suggestions on what to order? Our wings are a huge favorite."

Mattie's eyes lit at the mention of fried chicken wings. "Would you like some?"

Fortunately, he did because he never could have turned down the eagerness in her expression. "I do. Hot or mild?"

Together, they devoured a basket of moderately spicy wings and homemade chips. They watched the *Englischers*, who soon grew accustomed to their presence, and the place returned to laughter and happy conversation. Winston made up his mind to bring Mattie again, since she appeared as comfortable as he felt in the easy-going environment. By the time Dan returned to drive them home, whatever had upset Mattie at the seaside no longer seemed to be on her mind.

Even so, Winston pushed aside any thoughts of kissing her for the present time. He'd been rushing her. At least, that was his best guess at what had happened. The realization shamed him. Mattie deserved better. He could be a patient man.

After the van pulled up to the Bellers' house, Winston went to open the other door for Mattie. She stepped out and smiled up at him—an encouraging sign.

"*Danki*, Winston. I had a wonderful *goot* time." Her sky-blue eyes, so innocent and beguiling at the same time, drew him a step closer to her.

He took her right hand into his own. Her fingers were soft under his thumb as he pressed them gently. "I hope we can spend many more days together, Mattie."

He stepped back and let go of her hand before temptation overtook him. She turned to walk to her porch, then from the top stair rounded to watch him leave. He waved as his ride backed up to drive the other way to the Yoders'. The parting didn't square with the relationship he hoped was growing between them, leaving him with a desire to set things straight.

Soon, he'd have to tell her his heart had moved beyond friendship. Next time, he promised himself, would be different. And Mattie was worth the wait.

CHAPTER EIGHT

Days passed without a word from Winston. Mattie tried to push aside thoughts of him. And this morning she'd done better, until the weather turned her mind to the perfectness of this day for a winter stroll on the beach. But the phone had not rung or any buggy driven down the lane for her.

Winter solstice was less than a week away. The short days offered little light beyond the early afternoon—certainly no time for a trek to the shore.

Another opportunity was gone, and there was no sign another would be of any use. Yet she walked to the phone shed anyway to check the answering machine for messages. Winston had given her that one freeing moment with *Gott* to release her fear and rest in His hands. She hadn't been able to get the experience or Winston out of her thoughts ever since.

The door to the shed was open, and Mark stood inside. He turned around, holding the phone to his ear, then covered the mouthpiece with his hand. "No messages, Mattie, but Rachel is getting an order ready for *Datt*. Can you go pick it up?"

Mattie nodded. The ride from her farm to the vet's office was an easy one by scooter, unlike the uphill trek to the Yoders' the last time she had helped Rachel make a delivery. An asthma attack was unlikely on a day like today; besides, the distraction would be welcome.

Mark set the phone down. "She says it should be ready by the time you get there." Her brother fell into step beside her as she walked back to the house to fetch her scooter. "So, you do like this Winston fellow, eh?"

Mattie stopped and looked at the man beside her. How long until her own twin no longer resembled the Amish at all? She averted her gaze and kept walking, her attention focused on the gravel path under their feet. They'd never looked much alike, aside from their untamable curls, but they were family and always knew each other's minds. Until lately. Now, she wasn't sure she knew him at all.

"Do you really care, Mark?"

A firm tug at her elbow forced her to stop again. "I know the others will turn their backs on me, Mattie. But I didn't think you would, too."

"So, that's the way of it now. You speak badly of the people when no one has ever done you wrong, and yet you are the one leaving. As if nothing you do should merit any consequence. And, as always, if it does, then I am at fault. Holding you back from all the fun you could be having. Or, in this case, holding you responsible."

Ach, the bitterness of her words tasted foul on her tongue. Her brother's dark scowl proved there was no way to retrieve their poison either. She'd wounded her dearest friend.

"Ich binn sorry, bruder."

"Don't be sorry. I don't want to part ways like this—fighting. I don't expect your blessing on my choice, but I do wish you wouldn't be angry."

"I thought you were courting Ellen. I was preparing myself for when you moved away with her and started a new life. But leaving us . . . I never . . . "

"You weren't all wrong. When Ellen came, I did court her. I thought maybe I could make myself and everyone happy if things worked out between the two of us."

"You don't like her, then?"

"That's not it. She'll make a perfect *fraw* to an Amish man. I just can't be that man."

Who did he think he was, all of a sudden, other than an Amish man? Rather than ask, she walked faster to get her scooter and be gone. The ride would help clear her head. Nothing was making sense. Winston's silence. Mark's determination to be someone, something, anything not Amish.

She pushed her scooter a few feet from the house until her brother reached for the handle bars and stopped her. "You didn't answer my question about Winston."

She wasn't admitting anything when she hadn't even heard from Winston since their last outing.

"Thing is that word is getting around about your little snowmobiling excursion. You're right that I don't care, but *Datt* will find out sooner or later. I'd say it may be in your best interest to make it sooner and in your way of telling it." He let go of the handles. "And I do care about you and your happiness. First love doesn't last, Mattie. It's usually more of a practice run for the real thing. Best keep that in mind."

"Is that how you propose to let Ellen down easy?"

"I figure being the black sheep and scoundrel of the church will take care of it well enough for her."

Mattie's mouth dropped open. Her brother's stoic face was a façade. She clamped her mouth shut again. He didn't mean it, but poor Ellen. And Winston's low opinion of Mark was sure to dip even further.

"I better get going." She pushed off the ground with her left foot and steered away from Mark.

"Think about it, Mattie." Her brother's voice echoed down the lane.

Mark was right about talking to *Datt*. She just wished he'd take his own advice. As for his opinions on love . . . Well, he could keep those to himself.

The vet's office was located in a small, brick building. The parking lot was wedged between the building and the vet's house. Dr. Drake was an old bachelor, whose father before him had also been a veterinarian on the eastern shore of the island. The house and the office both appeared to Mattie as if they could have been around for both generations, plus a few more. But the inside of the office was always clean, mostly modern—at least the equipment seemed twenty-first century as far as she could tell—and smelled distinctly sterile.

Mattie pushed her scooter into the rack beside the front entrance with a sign that said Drake's Large Animal Hospital. She pulled the large glass door open and entered an empty waiting room. There was a small bell on top of the receptionist's desk, but Mattie felt reluctant to ring it. Instead, she picked up a well-read copy of the daily newspaper and sat in a chair closest to the staff door leading to the back of the office. Either Rachel or the secretary would come through that door eventually.

When Mattie first began coming here, Rachel had appeared out of place behind the counter wearing her Amish clothing, apron, and prayer *kapp*. Now, both the Amish and the islanders had grown accustomed to her presence here.

The fact their bishop had allowed Rachel to take the classes she needed to become a vet tech still amazed Mattie. She had to wonder if Dr. Drake had any idea what he had accomplished in convincing an Amish bishop to permit such a thing. But then, Bishop Nafziger wasn't like most Amish bishops. And Joel Yoder, his stepson, was already proving to be a very different kind of minister. She had hoped Joel's sensible ways and gentle preaching would be enough to keep Mark in the church. But Mark was making clear that his mind was made to leave.

For a while, Mattie's *datt* had restricted her friendship with Rachel out of fear Mattie might get some idea to follow in her footsteps. But over time, Rachel had proven to the church she was as committed to her faith as before. And then when it suited *Datt* for Mattie to help Rachel by picking up deliveries for him or their neighbors, nothing more had been said.

She very much doubted things would go as smoothly for Mark. *Datt* wouldn't allow it, if for no other reason than as an example to his other sons. And *Mamm* would be caught in the crossfire.

"Hello, Mattie." Rachel stood in the staff entryway, holding the door part-way open. "Can you come to the back? I have your *datt's* supplies ready."

Mattie followed Rachel and helped load the pile into a box she could fit in the scooter's basket. Dr. Drake bustled through the hallway, glancing their way and offering Mattie a quick smile with a nod.

"You must be busy, but the waiting room is empty."

"*Ya.* I have only a minute. We're getting ready to leave on an emergency call." Rachel ran a pencil down the checklist and then placed the receipt in the box before closing it. "I was hoping you'd come get the delivery, so I could talk to you about helping Lydia. She was so burdened when I saw her this morning. Her shop is always busy this time of year; and now with Ellen gone, she has no help with the children—not to even mention how she's supposed to keep the school running. And the school's Christmas Eve program is next week. *Ach, it's just all too much for her.*"

"Ellen's gone? I don't understand. Gone where?"

"*Ya,* she went home to Pennsylvania. I assumed you would know." Rachel's forehead wrinkled. "I am sorry. I don't have time to explain. But please consider it. You have a special way with children, and you would be an answer to prayer." Rachel handed the box to Mattie. She glanced at the back door, then to Mattie. "I have to go now. You can go back through the front. The door will lock behind you. Just think about what I said, please. Lydia hates to ask, but if you offered . . . " Rachel shrugged before sprinting down the hallway, where Dr. Drake was waiting.

Ellen was gone? Why?

Mattie hated to suspect her brother was at fault. And yet, his comments earlier would have broken any girl's heart.

Mattie hurried out the front with the box and secured it in the basket with bungee cords.

Did Winston leave as well, without saying goodbye? *First love never lasts.* Her brother's words whispered in her ear.

Mattie slumped against the brick wall for support and squeezed her eyes shut. *Breathe. Breathe.* Slower. Steady. *Breathe.* One, two, three, four. *Out.* Two, three, four. She reached into her pocket for her inhaler, flipped the cap, and pressed the plastic rim to her mouth. *Whoosh.*

The Lord is my salvation. I will not be afraid.[2]

Exhale.

---

2 Psalm 27:1

Wait on the LORD: be of good courage, and he shall strengthen thine heart: wait, I say, on the Lord.[3] She mentally quoted the verse she'd memorized to help her in moments like this.

The pain in her chest relaxed, and her lungs filled with air. She opened her eyes.

She could go inside and call Mark to get her.

Nay. She'd manage. The ride home wasn't hard.

She'd never been a fainting posy, not over any boy. And she wasn't going to act so ridiculous over a man she'd met less than two weeks ago.

First love? *Bah!* She had no explanation for why her body reacted so violently to the idea of Winston's leaving, but she wasn't about to call it love. Although, she was disappointed—unexpectedly much.

After a deep breath, Mattie straddled her scooter and turned toward home, determined to push aside memories of Winston or hopes for their next meetings. Purpose came by doing the next thing, so *Mamm* told her. Was the next thing to help Lydia take care of her children? Mattie did love them both—especially Samy, their daughter, who was kind, quirky, and dangerously honest. Surely, the school board wouldn't ask her to fill in as a teacher—not after she'd refused them once already.

Ya, she would help Lydia with Samy and Owen, as often as *Mamm* could spare her. She'd even mind the store, so Lydia could substitute at the school until Ellen returned.

As for the dreadful hill she'd have to climb to get there, she'd conquer it in the same way she was going to find her purpose—by putting one foot in front of the other. And maybe, she could forget Winston the same way.

---

3 Psalm 27:14

CHAPTER NINE

Saturdays on the dairy farm always included extra chores to make less work on the following Lord's Day. The cows required milking no matter the day, but other work could be done ahead to make Sunday easier. Since this week was a visiting Sunday falling so close to Christmas, she and *Mamm* would be busy all afternoon making cookies and candies to share. The youth planned to go to a local nursing home to sing for the residents, so Mattie was making extra to take along.

She reached for a baking dish on the countertop and pressed a fingertip lightly into the cooling caramel candy she'd poured earlier. Once ready, she'd cut this batch into small squares and wrap each one in wax paper. Finding the caramel both cool and firm, she flipped the pan upside down and used a silicone spatula to ease the contents in one large, rectangular block onto a wooden cutting board.

"Do you think we'll have enough?" She directed the question at her *mamm*, who was melting caramel to drizzle on top of marshmallow and graham cracker clusters, while Mattie cut her plain caramel candies with a butcher knife. "Maybe we need to pitch in some more, since Ellen won't be there."

"I have another idea. What if we invite the *youngies* here first, since our place is on the way?" *Mamm* lifted the top from the double boiler and began to pour the liquid over a tray filled with the cookie and marshmallow treats. "Everyone can come a little early, and we'll serve hot cocoa. While they visit with each other, they can also make cards to give to the elderly at the nursing home."

Mattie reached for a stack of cut wax paper.

"The cards are a *goot* idea, especially since some of the residents can't eat sweets." After she rolled a piece of caramel in the paper and twisted both ends closed, she placed it in a large bowl, which would soon be filled to overflowing. "Do you think we can get the word around to everyone in time?"

"When has spreading news been a problem?" *Mamm* laughed and tucked a wayward strand of her honey-blonde hair under her *kapp*. "If *Datt* can spare the horse and buggy, then you can go fetch some card-making supplies at Lydia's. She and Joel will help get the word out."

Mamm made a *goot* point. In less than twenty-four hours, the Bellers had heard the full story on Ellen and Winston's return to Pennsylvania. And no one seemed to think they were coming back either. *Datt* served on the school board and was in a dither over losing their teacher before the Christmas Eve program and only halfway through the year. No one had much to say about Winston. They must not have any reason to worry over his departure. If only Mattie could be as untouched by the loss of him.

Mattie surveyed all the work around her still to be done, keeping her mind distracted from thoughts of Winston. Mostly.

"I can't leave you with all this, *Mamm*."

"*Ya*, you can because I said so, Mattie Beller." *Mamm's* stern voice held no true reprimand. "Besides, this will give you an opportunity to speak with Lydia and find out how you can help." The playfulness on her *mamm's* face softened into compassion. "Things aren't always as they seem, *mei leeb*."

My love. Mamm's use of the endearment caused Mattie's eyes to mist.

"Go on now. The days are short. I'll get the boys to wrap those caramels." Her mother shooed her out the door with a coat, scarf, and a quick hug.

She found her father behind the barn stocking extra feed for the cows. Mark was helping carry the hundred-pound sacks of grain and insisted she wait a few minutes, so he could come with her.

As they walked away to get the horse and buggy, *Datt* called on them to wait.

"*Ya, Datt?*" she answered when they were closer to him.

He looked her in the eye, then pinned her brother with the same stare. "There's something I need to say to the both of you. You're my oldest children and both past due your time to leave the nest."

Mattie sucked in a breath. Their father rarely used this tone with them anymore—the one that meant they'd been found out—not since they were children.

She should have talked to him about the snowmobiling already. Beside her, Mark fidgeted and dug back and forth into the dirt with one foot. Mattie's spine stiffened with dread. Had *Datt* sniffed out his plans to leave? Or had her brother already told him?

But Mattie was the one caught in her father's stare now. "I haven't been in a hurry to see my only daughter married. It has been easy to think no one was *goot* enough for you. But one thing I know for sure is you won't find a *goot* Amish man if you go following the *Englisch* ways. You made your vow to the church, Mattie." His eyes flicked to her brother, a sure indication of his displeasure in not being able to say the same of his son. But then, his attention came back to her. "You're too old to be acting like you're in *Rumspringa*."

"*Datt!*" The force of Mark's interruption stunned Mattie as her brother stepped closer, coming between her and their father.

"An hour-long ride on the back of a snowmobile is not placing Mattie in danger of breaking her vows to her faith or to God. She never indulged in any kind of running around or *rumspringa* as a youth. In fact, she barely had any fun even when we were school children."

"Mark, please, stop." Mattie heard the begging in her plea, but her brother ignored her.

"Winston was the one man who saw beyond her shyness and insecurity and gave her an afternoon of pure excitement. Now, he's gone. Can't you let her have the memory without ruining it for her?"

Mark moved beside her again. "It's me who's disappointed you, *Datt,* not her."

Her twin was as different from her as Esau from Jacob, yet he had always read her heart and mind in a way she supposed only someone who'd known her from the womb could. Lately, she'd worried their bond was splintering, maybe about to break. And after the way he'd spoken to her the day before, she couldn't make sense of his sudden defense.

Mattie held her breath as she raised her head to look at their father, unsure what she would see. Anger? Humiliation? She couldn't bear either. As much as she loved her brother for defending her, she would never show *Datt* such disrespect.

Only her father's face was not to be seen. His back was to them. He called over his shoulder as he walked away, "You two had better get going before it gets late." Then he left them there.

"*Be ye angry, and sin not; let not the sun go down upon your wrath.*"[4] The Scripture floated through her mind in her *datt's* voice as she'd

---

4 Ephesians 4:26

heard them so many times. He did his best to live by those words. He was trying now, she knew.

"You were right, Mattie." Mark's voice jolted her. "I've put off talking to him for too long, and it's making things worse for him."

"We should make this visit to the Yoders a quick one. We can't leave *Datt* like this for long."

"Let me talk to him first, Mattie. I promise I'll do it tonight, first thing after dinner."

Mattie nodded. Why did everything have to happen all at once? Her favorite time of year was turning sour faster than scorched milk.

The road was slick, and Mark wished they had driven the sleigh instead. This snow was the perfect depth for the horses to manage the sleigh across the open fields. Still, the buggy was warmer for Mattie and it had headlamps if they got caught after dark. He'd just have to take it easy and slow. The mare knew what to do. He was not going to miss this complication of Amish life after he'd gone. Not in the slightest.

He was certain everyone was going to speculate he was the reason Ellen left in such a hurry. There was no way he was going to reveal her secret to save his own reputation—a reputation soon to be in shatters, anyway. But neither was he going to stand by and let Mattie take the heat for his choices.

The coming days were going to be unpleasant. *Datt* was usually reasonable; but when he felt like a failure, he had a terrible temper. Mark knew he'd walked away, rather than speak in anger.

"I didn't see your car back there in your hiding place." Mattie shivered, and he guessed it wasn't from the cold.

"That's why it's called a hiding place, Mattie." He waited for her to turn on him with one eyebrow pinched higher than the other.

Right on cue.

He laughed, and she swatted his arm.

"I sold it," he confessed.

Her mouth opened for so long, he was tempted to reach over and press it shut again. She leaned back against the seat, likely studying all the possible reasons for him to sell his car. That was her way. Eventually, he would tell her, and she would proclaim she already knew.

Mark chuckled.

"What's funny?"

"You are."

She turned away and looked out the window. She was lost deep in thought. He wasn't the only cause, either. Winston had been *goot* for her in the short time he'd been here. Mark suspected their *datt* had taken an instant liking to the fellow for that very reason. Mattie had a tendency to shut herself away from other people, but she'd been more open around Winston.

"I think he'll come back soon, Mattie."

"I'm afraid to wish for it."

"Why do you always sell yourself short? You have to know he cares for you. Everyone else can see it's so." Mark had to be cautious in how much he revealed without breaking Ellen's confidence, but he hated to see his sister so disappointed. "Winston didn't really have a choice except to help Ellen get home, not if he's a decent sort of man."

"I'm a terrible judge, you know, of this sort of thing."

"Are you saying you don't know how you feel about him?" Mark found the idea ridiculous. He'd never seen Mattie so eager to be with another person as she was to spend time with Winston.

"I'm saying it's best to be cautious because people will let you down."

He didn't have to think long to understand what fueled her fear. "Winston's not a schoolboy, Mattie. He's a grown man who has the sense to know he's found a good thing. And that is you." Mark cast a glance at her to assure she was listening. "Did you ever consider those boys were just cowards? They were afraid of you because they knew you were smarter."

"I'd be very prideful to think so."

"It's not pride to acknowledge simple facts." Mark wouldn't pry further. Mattie wasn't ready to share; besides, there was little else he could say.

"You sure have changed your tune since yesterday."

"I was upset, Mattie. Taking things out on you like that was wrong." Watching Winston fit into his family so well hadn't been easy when Mark was about to break away and lose that closeness. Still, he was happy for his sister. And he tried to take consolation in the hope that the strain with his family due to his choices wouldn't last forever. "I've gone about things in the wrong way. And I'm afraid it's going to get only worse before it gets better. I hope you'll be able to forgive me."

"I'll always forgive you, Mark. You know so."

If only he knew how to make everything right. He didn't. But he'd at least try to amend what little he could—first with Joel Yoder and later with his *datt*.

CHAPTER TEN

Dearest Mattie,

I hope you won't mind me calling you dearest, but I couldn't bring myself to write this letter to you in the same way I might address a business letter or an assigned pen pal from our school days. I'm not much of a letter writer. The only personal ones I've written since childhood are thank you notes. This is so much more important to me than a simple thank you. Please forgive me if I am no better with words than I was as a boy struggling to get through school.

As you will know by the time you read this, I am taking Ellen home. The timing is terrible, and I am sorry for it. I can't say I understand all of Ellen's reasons for leaving in such a hurry. Still, she is the closest of all my cousins, and there is no one else to help her.

I am afraid the bishop will say this is a sign I should never have come to New Hope. He thinks Bishop Nafziger and Joel are very progressive, and he does not approve. He and my parents both wanted me to get ideas of moving to the island out of my system. I'm certain things will not go well when I tell them I have become convinced otherwise in such a short time.

Still, I must trust *Gott*, His ways, and His timing in all things. Please pray for a miracle, Mattie. When I return to you, I wish to do so with my parents' blessing.

I will write to you when I have more news. There is no need for you to write back. Your letters may not reach me, as I cannot say when I will leave Lancaster. I hope for it to be very soon.

Until then, I will keep you close in both my thoughts and prayers.

Humbly Yours,

W.S.

With hands chilled by the morning air, Mattie folded the letter and slipped it back into her apron pocket before the brisk wind carried it out of her grasp. She'd read the contents more than a dozen times since Lydia had given it to her the previous day. Wrapping her arms around the ropes which held her beloved swing, she leaned back as far as the seat permitted without dumping her off to the ground.

The sky, visible through the barren branches of the maple which held her, was a perfect clear blue this Lord's Day. Her nose and cheeks burned from the cold wind. As she repositioned her scarf to protect the lower part of her face, her breath quickly warmed her covered skin. She closed her eyes, then lifted her feet, and pumped the swing in a soothing motion—not high but gentle above the ground—above her worry.

This cold winter air calls with powerful feeling.[5] The words of the children's rhyme came to mind. Silly as she must sound as a grown woman, no one was listening, so she sang the old words of her childhood.

---

5 Joachim Neander, *In der Stillen Einsamkeit,* 17th century German Reformation hymn. English translation, Amy Grochowski.

In der Stillen Einsamkeit

Findest du mein lob bereit.

Grosser Gott erhöre mich,

Denn mein herze suchet Dich.

~

In the silent loneliness

Discover Thou my willing praise.

Holy God hear Thou me

For my heart is seeking Thee.[6]

As often as she had sung this song, the lonesome words never stabbed as keenly as when they crossed her lips now. Was she lonely for Winston? *Ya*, she admitted to herself.

Before, she'd always thought the songwriter felt isolated because *Gott* was silent, and then later in the song, he found *Gott's* voice and presence in His creation. *Behold, what a mighty Lord! Summer and winter He makes.* The final words echoed.

As a child, the lesson from the song was always to understand *Gott's* power and constancy to sustain all things in order. Had the author also been lonely for human relationships and found comfort from *Gott* through nature?

Mattie's memory flew to the day Winston took her snowmobiling. He'd wanted her to experience *Gott* through nature, the way he had when skiing down a mountainside in Montana. Now, Winston was gone. But *Gott* had met her in the same way on her swing—His Holy Spirit ordering peace in her anxious heart.

---

6 Ibid.

The steady staccato of horses' hooves came from far off. Mattie opened her eyes. Before she'd left the house to walk to her swing, her father had told her the other members of the school board, as well as Bishop Nafziger and Joel Yoder, were coming to discuss solutions for their need for another teacher.

Four extra buggies would line her family's lot soon. *Mamm* was likely already percolating fresh *kaffi* on the stove and expecting Mattie to help serve the hot beverage, along with the tray of meats and cheeses they'd prepared for the guests. As the swing descended toward the ground, she released her grip on the ropes and jumped from the seat.

She hadn't consciously been seeking *Gott* when she'd come to her quiet place to swing; but as she walked back toward the house, the revelation that He'd sought her almost took her breath away. He'd come in her solitude, eased her worry, and comforted her with the gentle reminder of His presence.

How often had He come before, yet she'd been too full of her own thoughts to listen? Even plain, living a simple life, she had to be careful not to crowd *Gott* out of her heart and mind.

Ach, but she was thankful for the quiet moment alone this morning. *Danki, Gott, for preparing my heart to face whatever today may bring. Help me listen to Your Spirit and follow Your Word.*

Back in her mother's kitchen, Mattie sliced thick pieces of bread for sandwiches, while her mother set the table. The yeasty aroma of the loaves baked the previous day still filled the air. The German pumpernickel rye her father preferred combined with her mother's well-known oatmeal loaf created a mouth-watering temptation beside the cold ham, beef, and farmer's cheese made from their own dairy.

After arranging the tray on the dining table next to jars of home-canned pickles and applesauce, Mattie stood back, pleased with the bountiful offering for their visitors. The men's voices drifted from the living room, sometimes muffled and other times jovial. But for several minutes, their low whispers had become indecipherable.

She tried not to eavesdrop; but the more the men concealed their conversation, the more her curiosity sparked. She had heard enough to know they were considering using substitutes to finish out the current school year. Fortunately, she had already volunteered her services to Lydia, which gave her a valid excuse to stay off the substitute list. But after the busy Christmas season, Lydia wouldn't need her anymore.

Mattie groaned.

She'd be hard-pressed to obtain an exemption from her community duty and responsibility for the remaining months. Serving as a temporary substitute wouldn't be so bad. Only, she suspected temporary would lead to permanent and snuff out the little hope which remained for something more with Winston. Her teacher in Ontario had been an old maid, a forever maid the children called her because she never married.

"Mattie!"

She jumped at her *datt's* voice, as if he knew she was straining to hear his conversation.

"*Dochtah, kumm rei.*"

A glance at her *mamm* revealed a knowing grin, followed by a nod to follow her *datt's* call to come into the meeting. Mattie reminded herself that unlike *Mamm*, her father was not a mind-reader. She straightened her apron and entered the next room.

"*Ya, Datt.* I'm here."

Winston's long journey with Ellen by bus, then train, and finally a local driver from the station to his parents' house was over at last. Ellen went into the house, while he walked across the way and entered his father's workshop through the side entrance.

His father co-owned the business with Winston's uncle Amos. Winston's *datt*, Jeremiah, was the manager. Uncle Amos was a gifted carpenter. Together, the brothers had built a manufacturing giant that sold Amish-made sheds in every state east of the Mississippi, plus Ontario. Winston had become their top salesman, and business was quickly expanding west.

All the money he earned before turning twenty-one had gone directly to his father and mother, as was their church custom. Unlike many others in the district, his family saved the money their children earned as a gift to finance their future after they joined the church. Most of Winston's friends never saw their hard-earned cash. Paychecks were handed over and the funds spent as the parents saw fit. Of course, many of those families weren't as blessed with money as the Stoltzfus family.

While he'd done very well over the past year in his father's business, he was counting on his other savings to invest in the purchase of a home on the island. Up until now, he hadn't been overly worried. But then, he hadn't planned on also supporting a wife.

He'd hoped for peace with his parents over his choice, but if the worst happened, he'd make do. He could use his own savings and apply for a Canadian work visa. He'd live on a meager subsistence until he got on his feet and invest the rest in the sugar maple farm and orchard he dreamed of owning.

He'd had everything figured out—until he met Mattie.

Now, he not only needed the money his parents had saved, but he also wouldn't feel right to begin a marriage without their blessing. And he couldn't imagine living on the island without Mattie by his side.

The small office that partitioned off one corner of the building was cold. No one had any reason to heat the office on a Sunday. Winston emptied his pockets of a few receipts and the business cell phone. He opened the top drawer of his father's desk, where the phone was kept, then slipped the receipts into an envelope for safekeeping.

With a reluctant push, he closed the drawer. How many times had he almost called Mattie over the past few days? He'd lost track. He didn't understand what was holding him back. He missed Mattie with a deep ache. Was he afraid to hear her voice, while he was so uncertain when he'd see her again? Maybe that was it. Talking to her when he couldn't see her would just make the coming days more unbearable. He would keep his promise to write to Mattie—just as soon as he had anything new to tell her.

Leaving the building, the heavy door clicked behind him. He paused, the key ready in his hand. For the first time, the reality of how very far he'd been separated from the realization of his dreams struck him, and he couldn't bring himself to turn the lock.

Halfway between the office and his family home, dark storm clouds released a downpour of bone chilling, cold rain. He yanked his black coat over his head and ran. By the time he reached the covered porch of the house, his clothes were soaked. He wiped the water dripping down his face and shook out the coat.

Draping his wet coat on a peg rather than drag a wet mess into the house, he noticed his aunt's buggy. She sure hadn't taken long, undoubtedly eager to whisk Ellen home before too many busybodies got to her.

Ellen's troubles complicated everything. She'd waited until they were almost home before explaining that she was in the family way and had come home to make the father do right by marrying her. She was trying to pretend everything was normal. Perhaps, she thought she could somehow hurry up a wedding, and no one ever know.

He wished, for her sake, things might be so easily fixed. But once she'd pointed out her troubles, even Winston could see why she'd left in a hurry. The time for hiding her condition would soon be past.

He braced himself before entering his parents' home.

Whatever happened with Ellen would affect his family deeply, especially his *mamm*. The last thing he wanted to do was cause any more emotional turmoil. Announcing his heart had found a new home was a sure-fire way to do that very thing.

"Winston!" Ellen greeted him with over-the-top enthusiasm for someone who'd spent the past three days crammed beside him on buses and a train. "We were just saying goodbye." Underneath her great effort to appear positive, Winston knew his cousin was frightened. He wanted to help, but she refused to confide a single detail to him—not even the name of the father.

"Welcome home, son." His father's face was grave and his *mamm's* possibly more ashen. Winston nodded at his *datt* and walked over to place an arm around his mother's shoulders.

His aunt gave him a curt hello, then tugged at Ellen's arm. "We'll be going."

Ellen made no sign of submitting to her mother's rush.

"*Danki*, Winston. I'm sorry to have interrupted your visit to New Hope." She paused and shifted her gaze directly to his parents. "It would be a shame if you didn't get back to Mattie and very soon."

"*Kumm!*" His aunt wasn't waiting another minute. Ellen followed her out the door.

"Winston?" His *mamm* broke the short silence after his cousin's departure. Her sweet gray eyes looked up to him. "Who's Mattie?"

The best response evaded him. He hadn't even had time to ask Mattie how she felt toward him. He wanted to believe she was drawn to him in return. When he was with her last, he wasn't certain she felt the same as he did. They still hadn't talked about their evolving friendship. What if she didn't want more?

Rushing forward with his plan to move began to seem more and more foolish. But if not now, when?

Mattie stood in her living room, facing the waiting stares of her father, minister, bishop, and the two other school board members. *Datt* hadn't *asked* her to be the teacher for their one-room school. He'd told her. She was their choice, and he left no doubt he expected her to accept.

Danki, brother, for picking last night to talk to Datt. Mark always had such poor timing. At least *Mamm* didn't seem to know—yet.

Her father gave her a look that brooked no argument. Joel Yoder appeared sympathetic, as if offering her courage. The bishop maintained an impartial mask, while both Ben Hostettler and David Friesen glanced nervously around the room.

"Mattie?" The question in her father's tone pushed her to answer. He'd never spoken to her in such a demanding way. And she had never disappointed him. Except for the snowmobile incident. Was this her punishment?

Her lungs constricted. She had no air to answer, even if she knew what to say.

At her age, becoming a school teacher was a sure sign she'd never marry. Only a few weeks ago, she'd been convinced she had no desire for marriage. This second chance to be their teacher might have come like an answer to her prayer to find a purpose in her community—a way to serve the Lord.

But now, she hoped . . .

"I'd like to speak with Mattie. Alone." Bishop Nafziger was on his feet. He nodded at her. "*Kumm,* child. Sit and talk to me while the others go to eat."

The bishop's gentle eyes never left her as she was seated, and one by one, the men made their way to the next room. Whatever was bothering her *datt,* he wouldn't undermine the bishop's authority.

Her pulse quickened in her chest, despite her knowledge of the man as a kind and patient elder. She'd never been alone with the bishop and feared what she may have done to get so much attention.

"David speaks well of your ability to teach. It would seem even as a young *maydel,* you helped him to learn his studies in school. Is this so?"

She nodded slowly. David was years ahead of her in school. She always believed he'd been upset their teacher had assigned Mattie to help him with mathematics.

"Ben and Joel have both witnessed your *goot* sense and patience with their children. They say you understand the *kinder* and know how to maintain order with kindness."

She swallowed, thankful he hadn't asked for her verification of those opinions. Although, the knowledge Ben and Joel thought well of her did ease her tension—enough so that she could lift her eyes back to the bishop's grandfatherly face.

"All these things are important to our parents. Most of all, our want is for a teacher who will guide our children through her own faithfulness."

Of its own volition, her head dropped. "I'm sorry . . . about the snowmobile." If only she could express how the experience drew her closer to *Gott,* not away from Him.

A soft pressure squeezed her shoulder. The bishop's weathered hand rested there for a moment. His eyes drew her head back up, and then he removed his touch. "It was not a sin and has done no harm to the community. There is no prohibition against riding a snowmobile, only in owning one."

"*Datt* did not like it."

"Then you must make things right with your father, *ya?*"

How had she not done so already? "*Ya.* I will."

"Very *goot.* And then, you will think and pray on our great need for a teacher and whether *Gott* desires you to use your abilities to serve in this way?"

How often had she been taught from the Scripture that a person's gifts belong to the Lord? Only the Sunday past, Joel had preached so. Would she be burying the talents the Lord had given her by refusing to help?

And then she knew what she must do, for the Spirit was calling. She could not deny Him. "*Ya*, I will do it."

The bishop's eyes brightened, and his brow lifted in question.

"I mean, I will teach the children." *Ach*, but she was afraid. For all the talents she possessed, she had far more shortcomings. "And you will pray for me? Please. I don't know what I'm doing."

"*Gott's* strength is made perfect in weakness, ain't so?" The bishop stood to his feet, and she followed his lead. "For now, you can focus on the Christmas program. You already know everything you need to lead the children in their presentations. And Lydia will help train you in the rest. Come summer, we can send you to conference with other Amish teachers. Just remember, you must rely on *Gott's* wisdom, not your own."

And just like that, her fate was sealed. She'd never marry and would probably set a record for the longest-serving Amish school teacher of all time.

A few weeks ago, she'd have been thrilled to have a purpose. But now? She sensed another desire slipping through her grasp—a sacrifice of something not quite yet her own. Deep in her heart, she knew she made the right choice—willingly. Why, then, was a part of her so unhappy?

Everyone else in the crowded kitchen was jovial. The men joked as men do when a heavy burden has been lifted. The boys, her brothers, waited in high spirits for the pie about to be served. Only *Mamm* noticed Mattie's melancholy. Mattie knew because her mother pulled her by the hand to the far corner of the room.

"Patience, Mattie. *Gott* works all things out for the *goot* of those who love and serve Him.[7] *Ya?*"

---

7 Romans 8:28

Mattie nodded. She hoped so, at least.

"You get the *kaffi*. And remember, *Gott* loves a cheerful giver."[8] A tender smile spread on her *mamm's* face, so that Mattie felt no rebuke from her words. *Mamm's* cheerfulness was contagious and wrapped around Mattie like a hug.

She was right. If Mattie was going to teach the children and put on their Christmas program, she'd do so with a happy heart. And maybe—just maybe—Winston would be back in time to see it.

She reached for the coffeepot and noticed the last slice of shoofly pie beside the stove. Mark's favorite.

Scanning the room to see if her brother had a piece, his absence was apparent. Is this how it would be after Christmas? He'd leave, and she'd find herself always looking for him where he ought to be. She felt the emptiness in the pit of her stomach.

First Ellen, and soon, Mark would be gone as well.

Dear Gott, please let Winston return, even if only as a friend.

---

8 2 Corinthians 9:7

CHAPTER ELEVEN

Early the next morning, Lydia met Mattie at the schoolhouse a half-hour before the students were to arrive. Smoke drifted upward from the chimney, and a moderately warm room greeted them when they entered.

"Joel will come and start the fire before breakfast when he can. That way, you won't be freezing. We'll stoke it and have a *goot* warm fire by the time the children arrive." Lydia placed the basket on her arm by the teacher's desk, then made a straight path to the wood stove, opened it, and tossed in some more split logs. "At the end of the day, we'll have one of the boys re-stock the woodpile here from the storage out back, while one of the girls cleans the blackboard. They're easy chores all of the children are capable of doing, so we'll rotate the assignment each day. When the supply of split wood gets low, either Michael or Jude can do the job of splitting some more."

Mattie shook her head in understanding. Her brother, Michael, and Jude were the two oldest boys in the school and well-acquainted with the work of an axe and a woodpile. And the families of the church all pitched in with a steady supply of wood-burning logs.

"On very cold days, Joel can bring a kerosene heater to help keep the room warm. But if it's too cold for the woodstove to keep the children warm enough, then it's also too cold for them to walk to school, so I don't think you'll have much need for an additional heater."

Because her *datt* was on the school board, Mattie knew they planned to install a safer secondary heating system as soon as they had the funds. Of course, in such a small district, everyone else knew all the school business, too.

"We'll make do. Tell Joel *danki* for starting the fire for us." Mattie suspected he'd done the same for Ellen, but the warm air would help her catch her breath after the cold walk, so she was doubly grateful.

"I want you to know how much I appreciate your offer to help me with the children and the shop. But this is a far greater need—not only to me but for all of us."

"As long as I don't mess it up."

Lydia laughed. "You won't. You'll see."

If only Mattie were so confident.

The schoolroom appeared similar to the one Mattie had attended in Ontario. However, Lydia and Ellen were both from Lancaster, and some of the differences showed. The parents, the school board, and the teacher all worked together to make their new school in the New Hope district work for the future needs of the children, as well as their parents and the church's collective values. The community was excited by the end result, and the school year began on a high note of enthusiasm for everyone.

Above the blackboard, she recognized the sign Mark had made, which read, "Study to show thyself approved unto a God, a workman that needeth not to be ashamed (2 Timothy 2:15)."

She would do her best to help the school year end as well as it had begun. With *Gott's* help.

The walls were uncluttered. Only a few charts and study tools had been posted in sight of the student desks, lined in columns on the left side of the room. Two bookshelves stood against the wall behind the desks and were lined with rows of storybooks for reading when assigned work was completed.

To the right of the blackboard was the teacher's desk—a large table with drawers on each side of her straight-backed chair. On top was a stapler, a jar filled with pencils, and a hand-crank pencil sharpener. In front of the teacher's desk, three tables were arranged in a u-shape with chairs facing the teacher for special instruction, based on age and grade level, while the other grades learned by self-study, guided through books and worksheets, until their group was called.

Mattie felt sure whatever had caused Ellen to leave in a hurry must have been unavoidable. Her careful and diligent touch was visible in every aspect of the room. Why would she leave all her efforts behind? Mattie pushed the question to the back of her mind. None of the possibilities she imagined were pleasant. She missed Winston but thanked *Gott* he was with her friend to help her.

"*Kumm*," Lydia called from the teacher's desk. "I have samples of each child's work, so you can see where they are in their studies."

Soon, laughter drifted from the playground outside, announcing the students' arrival.

Lydia looked up from the workbooks and texts she was showing Mattie. She smiled.

"Are you ready?"

Mattie looked at the clock above the doorway. Eight on the dot.

"Ready as I can be."

Mattie smoothed her apron with both hands and crossed the room to the closed door. She closed her eyes momentarily, took a deep breath, and then she opened the door and called for the children in clear English. Unless she was teaching German, she would use only English, so the children would learn to speak well in the language they needed for business and other interactions with the world. Her example in all things was paramount, and the responsibility weighed heavy on her.

" . . . eighteen, nineteen . . . " She counted aloud as the boys and girls filed past, reinforcing the order and pronunciation of the numbers to the youngest ones. "Twenty . . . "

Ten-year-old Floyd Friesen stopped in front of her with a paper note held out. "Merry's sick."

Mattie bent her knees at a slight angle to come face-to-face with the tow-headed boy. He'd be taller than her in a few years. "I'm sorry. We will pray for her to get well soon."

The boy nodded and went to his seat, followed by the last two students. Twenty-three students, including little Merry, made up the sum of their school.

Michael squirmed in his seat, likely uncomfortable being under his sister's authority. He wouldn't shame her, though—that she knew well. Besides, he only had to finish out this term before he was done with school altogether. He'd survive.

Her little brothers sat tall, maybe somewhat proud. She'd have to make sure they didn't act as if they were better than the other children because their sister was the teacher. They'd learn soon enough that everyone was equal in their classroom.

Mattie was thankful for Lydia's presence at the school throughout the morning. By lunchtime, however, she insisted Lydia could return home to open her shop for business the rest of the day.

The afternoon began with math and plenty of groans.

"Today we are going to play a game with number patterns." In her school days, Mattie thought the teacher ought to make math more fun. Numbers were exciting, and she hoped the children would begin to look forward to math, at least some of them.

She divided the room into four teams, encouraging the children to think through the assignments with her, so that each team was fairly divided by number and combination of ages. The exercise was quick to show how serious most of her students took a challenge, along with distinguishing the leaders from the followers.

"All right, children. The goal is to help each person on your team do his or her very best. You are not to compare yourself to the other teams but focus on completing your problems well and together. Does everyone understand the rules?"

Heads nodded, and twenty-two pairs of eyes gleamed with excitement. Michael's mouth hung open, as if he didn't recognize his sister in his new teacher at all. The first graders bounced with as much confidence as the older children exuded with squared shoulders and ready stance to take the first turn at the chalkboard.

"The prize for cooperation and diligent work will be a short extra recess before rehearsal for the Christmas program." Mattie's announcement was met by cheers. She cast a glance to each team. "Ready?" The leaders gave her curt nods. "Go!"

By the end of the day, Mattie was tired, yet surprisingly satisfied. Why had she ever been so afraid to be a teacher? She felt as if she were made for this work.

"Mattie?" Michael waited at the door with their three youngest brothers bundled in their black winter coats, felt hats, and leather boots. "Should we wait for you?"

"*Nay*, go on home. I'll be right behind you."

"All right." He opened the door, then looked back at her. "It's starting to snow right heavy, Mattie. Sure you'll be coming soon?"

"*Ya*, Michael, I'll be fine." She attempted to soothe her brother's concern.

He glanced at the replenished woodpile. Seeming satisfied, he closed the door behind him.

A few days ago, Michael wouldn't have noticed her if she ran through the house naked. She smiled. *Ya*, being a teacher was a *goot* way for her to do her part in *Gott's* work at New Hope.

Before going to bed the previous day, she'd made a point to go to her *datt* about his displeasure with her snowboarding. He told her his worry was how the rumor circulating among the people might affect her chances of being their teacher. Although, he clarified, if Winston were still around, he may have a bit to say to him on the matter. And now, Mattie wondered if her father understood something more about her than she knew herself. At the very least, he was correct in his belief that teaching would suit her—more than she imagined possible.

And she would do her best to be a *goot* teacher for the children, beginning by correcting the morning work assignments and planning the next day's lessons. The fire would be out soon, but her work wouldn't take long, so she left it alone.

Before long, the light from the windows dimmed, so that she fired up a propane lantern to see better. Her stomach panged with a longing for supper—a bit earlier than usual, so she worked steady until the sensation stopped.

As she stacked all the papers into a neat pile for the next day, a puff of her breath clouded in the chilled air. How had the room cooled so fast? She looked up at the clock, but the room was too dark to see the time. Grabbing the lantern, she first looked out the window. Black as coal. Closer to the clock, she lifted the lantern high. Six-thirty?

She opened the door and was greeted by more than a foot of snow on the small porch. Was the snow deeper on the ground? The fact the previously shoveled steps had disappeared affirmed the possibility. The light from the lantern illuminated a fast and strong snowfall still coming down. She stepped back and shoved the door shut against the drift.

Her trembling hands made re-starting the fire difficult. Smoke filled her nostrils before she could turn her head. Using her left hand, she pulled her apron up to her face to filter the air. Still, she coughed.

She willed her fear aside before panic helped induce an asthmatic fit. There was enough wood to keep her warm until someone came. Because someone would come. They had to.

"Son, stop!" Mark heard his father call through the white wall of snow falling between the two of them with the horse and harness in between. He felt a tug on the reins in his hand. "Going off and getting killed won't solve anything or put things right."

"What if she's not safe in the schoolhouse, *Datt*? What if she's lost in this storm?" Their brother had said Mattie told him she'd be coming right along. Hours ago. And Mark was the reason they hadn't noticed she was so late. He and his father had been consumed by Mark's revelations. The whole rotten lot of them.

Ellen was pregnant with another man's child. In hurt and anger— and maybe a little bit of a push to go ahead with a plan he'd contemplated without true intention—Mark had run off and signed up to join the Canadian Royal Air Force. He'd sold his car to give Ellen enough money to get home, so her family could help her. And now, he had no way out of the contract with the military, no matter if he regretted his haste.

The mixture of horror and crushing defeat on his *datt's* face was a heart-rending sight burned on his conscience forever. It made little difference that the military desired Mark's natural genius for numbers, complex memorization, and riddle-solving skills for use in intelligence to save lives, not take them. He wasn't a warrior. They wanted his brain. And not only would they pay him well, but also his education would be funded so he could learn to do things he'd thought possible only in science fiction. None of those things would comfort his *datt*. In fact, all of those things were of the world from which his father worked so hard to protect him.

Somehow, his father managed to ease the reins from Mark's grip. And then, the strong arms of the man who'd raised him—who loved him against all odds—wrapped around his shoulders and pulled him into a tight embrace.

If not for his fear for his sister, Mark might be reduced to weeping right now. In all his life, his father had not hugged him. The power of his hold in this moment outdid the intensity of their previous pain and disagreement.

His father pulled back, keeping hold of Mark's arms. "Go to the shanty and call Joel. May the *goot* Lord let him hear the phone in his barn. He is much closer and can check the school to see if Mattie is there. If he cannot, we will call the authorities." He released Mark and then pushed a large battery-operated flashlight into his hands. "Be careful. You will do as I ask, *ya?*"

"Yes, *Datt.* I will come back to the house as soon as I get a return call from Joel." Assuming Joel answered and found Mattie safe at the school.

This was the worst blizzard he'd seen on the island and by far the earliest. Truth be told, he wasn't sure the local authorities could even find Mattie until the snow let up. Joel was their best hope. And he prayed that she'd stayed put in that small but heated school for shelter.

If Joel didn't answer, Mark wouldn't hesitate a minute to call emergency services. And for once, he didn't think his Amish church and family would disagree with his judgment.

CHAPTER TWELVE

We read of a place that's called heaven,
It's made for the pure and the free;
These truths in God's Word He hath given,
How beautiful heaven must be.[9]

Never in his life had a hymn sounded as sweet as the faint song carried to Winston's listening ears on this frozen night.

He and Joel had planned their strategy for a search in a hurry. They ruled out using the horses. Amazon may have cleared the deep snow in most places, but neither of them were comfortable risking the possibility of taking the horse into deep drifts. Instead, they opted for the two pairs of snowshoes, poles to check the depth as they walked, and a sleigh for Mattie.

The snowfall and blowing wind eased about a hundred or so yards earlier. By the landmarks they'd been able to locate, the school had to be close.

Encouraged by the distant sound, and hopeful it was truly Mattie's voice, he scanned the horizon with a flood light Joel had rigged to a battery to help their search. A whiff of burning firewood indicated the singing hadn't been his imagination. He held the light up again and caught a reflection from a window less than twenty feet ahead of them. Then higher above the roof, he illuminated the tell-tale smoke from the chimney—evidence Mattie was safe inside.

---

9 A.S. Bridgewater, *How Beautiful Heaven Must Be*, 1920, Public Domain, https://hymnary.org/text/we_read_of_a_place_thats_called_heaven.

"The Lord be praised." Joel clamped a steady hand on Winston's shoulder. "I can follow our tracks back with the small flashlight. You get Mattie, while I call the Bellers to let them know all is well."

Before Mark calls for an emergency rescue.

Winston understood what Joel left unsaid.

Mattie's brother had been frantic with worry by the time Winston heard his messages and called back. And Winston was right there on the verge of craziness himself after hearing how long Mattie had been alone at the school or possibly lost in the storm.

"Go ahead. We'll be right behind you."

He knew the man was as thankful as he was this rescue trip was going better than they hoped. They'd done all they could. And *Gott* took care of the rest.

"I imagine that will depend on how warm things are inside that schoolhouse." Joel laughed. "You two might have some talking to do. But don't stall long and make Lydia worry over much, *ya?*"

Winston's mouth dropped open. Did all ministers have an uncanny ability to read minds? Winston hadn't shared his feelings for Mattie with anyone. She'd be the first to hear it from him. And soon.

Joel had already turned back before Winston could formulate a response. Her family deserved to know—as soon as possible—how they'd discovered her singing in the schoolhouse with a fire to keep her warm.

Winston lunged into a sprint over the short distance remaining, as fast as the snowshoes allowed, while also tugging the sleigh loaded with a shovel, blankets, and a thermos of piping hot cocoa. The light shone over the top of at least three feet of snow as he hastened one foot in front of the other all the way to the front door.

The melody of another tune greeted him, so he pushed the door open, rather than knock. He didn't want her to stop yet. Her voice was gentle, clear, and powerful as she controlled each note's strength as if on a wave across the dim room.

He stood mesmerized—until she stopped, and he realized he hadn't seen her yet. Only the low light of a lantern appeared on a desk close to the stove.

Where was she?

His fingers found the switch on the floodlight. He flicked it. The unexpected brightness was followed by a sharp squeal and sudden thud.

"Ouch!"

Her voice came from near the desk. Was she under there?

"Mattie? Where are you?"

"Is that you? Winston?" His name rang on a note of disappointment. Not the reaction he expected. Surely not what he returned to the island for in such a hurry.

"*Ya.* It's me." He walked to the voice and peeked around the large desk.

There she was—on the floor, with one arm wrapped around her knees and the other rubbing her head—huddled under the teacher's desk. Slowly, she lifted her face to him. "That hurt."

Relief flooded through his veins. He breathed easy for the first time since he'd set off to answer the mysterious phone call in the barn. She was well and whole, except for the bump to her head after he'd startled her. And heavens, was she ever beautiful.

He left the light on the floor and reached to help her. With ease, he pulled her from under the desk, then heaved her up with both hands. She stumbled forward into his chest.

He was about to ask what in the world she was doing under the desk. Suddenly, he didn't care. Instead, he slid his arms from his hold on her elbows to wrap around her waist. When she didn't pull away, he let a hand slip to her forehead to touch a loose curl of her hair.

She sucked in a short breath.

"Is that where you hit your head?"

"*Nay.*"

"I'm sorry about that."

Her hands came up and rested on his chest, and he felt very forgiven.

When she tilted her head upward, he was undone. He cupped her flushed cheek with his hand. Still, he took pause to be sure she was asking.

Her open lips were all the assurance he needed, and all the waiting he could bear had long since passed.

If Winston didn't kiss her soon, Mattie was going to wish the ceiling had collapsed on her head after all. Why didn't he get on with it?

All her astonishment that he was back and the mortification of being found in such a state vanished the second he'd wrapped his arms around her. She nestled deeper into the warmth he offered.

He groaned. Just a little. And the sound sent a shiver up her spine. The delicious kind. Then heaven spilled over when his lips met hers.

He pulled back, making her thirsty again. This time for more of his touch. She pressed onto her toes and pulled him down for another kiss. Longer. Deeper. And she understood how much he'd been holding back the first time. She'd never kissed a man; and in this moment, she never wanted to stop.

Winston broke the contact and leaned his forehead against hers. His breathing was rough. "We have to get back to the Yoders'. Everyone is worried sick about you. And the storm could worsen again."

She let her hands fall back to her sides. A smile remained on her lips, despite her reluctance to let him go.

"*Danki* for coming." Not only for finding her but for returning to her—to New Hope. Would he comprehend all she meant?

He smiled and ran a finger along her chin, his touch so tender, her heart might melt, despite the cold. His hand fell, and he entwined his fingers with hers. "*Kumm*, I have a sleigh for you. And Lydia sent wool blankets and hot cocoa to keep you warm."

As he readied the sled, she recalled his breathing had been more ragged than her own. Her heart was all a flutter, but her lungs were working perfectly.

Kissing, it turned out, was terrific exercise for an asthmatic.

CHAPTER THIRTEEN

Mattie woke with a slow realization she was not at home. Eyes still closed, she snuggled tighter under the quilt and heavy blankets in the Yoders' third-floor guest room. They'd renovated their home from an old boarding school with extra rooms, plus drafts aplenty, on this floor. Lydia had been right about needing these extra blankets.

Slowly, she uncovered her head and opened one eye at a time. Still, the sudden brightness caused her to squint. The bold colors of sunrise streaked across the high sky. The storm must have passed.

Her socked feet hit the floor, and she wrapped the top quilt around her shoulders. Closer to the window, the vivid reds of the horizon came into view, soon followed by an endless landscape of pure white, as if the ground had swollen and buried everything six feet below a magical new world.

She pressed a cheek against the cold glass and strained to make out the school in the distance. If not for the stub of a bell tower, the roof would blend directly into the snow like a small hill. Indeed, the Lord had granted a very narrow break in the blizzard for her rescuers. And praise *Gott*, the roof still had not collapsed.

A flush of warmth crept over her at the recollection of her fear and how she'd been found closeted under her desk for protection. *Ach*, Winston. Delight tickled her spine at the memory of the intimacy they'd shared. A kiss, then two. And before she'd even breathed her morning prayers, here she was wishing for a third.

She knelt at the window sill. The floor chilled her knees, spurring her on to pray. This morning didn't require a prayer book for inspiration. Instead, gratitude and praise poured straight from her heart to the One Who had given her so much. *And please, Gott, give me wisdom to go forward in a way that is goot in Your sight. Amen.*

She made the bed and dressed as quickly as possible. Anxious for warmth, she brushed her hair and pinned the wild curls under her prayer *kapp* before racing down the stairs.

"Whoa, there." Winston met her at the bottom of the stairwell.

She came to an abrupt stop.

He radiated cold and smelled of melted snow, likely from shoveling a path to the barn. He and Joel would've been up for a long spell taking care of the animals.

"*Gude mariye,* Winston." Her voice came out all giddy. She looked away in an attempt to regain some composure. He might be in want of a good thawing, but she was more than warm enough for them both. After last night, how was she to be herself?

She felt the nudge of Winston's forefinger crooked under her chin, bringing her back to face him. His eyes met hers, and she thought he might steal a kiss.

"Glad to see you have your color back," he offered instead.

Ya, a lot of color and growing exponentially under his watchfulness. "Very funny." She pushed around him. "I hear breakfast sizzling."

She focused on making her way to the kitchen and ignored the chuckle behind her. Or at least, she hid the grin threatening to undo her pretend earnestness to get away from him. Besides, she should have been up long ago to help Lydia.

He called from a few feet behind her. "You're going to be stuck here for a while, you know . . . with me."

Ya, she knew all right, but she wasn't about to give away how the idea thrilled her. Terrified her, even. He'd stolen her heart and her first kiss, but he was still a visitor. And she'd discovered how much she also loved being a teacher. One future was certain, the other might only be a dream.

Before long, the kitchen was crowded with six hungry early-risers. The two children waited on the bench seat at the back of the table; then Joel came from the washroom to sit at the head of the table. Winston squished onto the bench. Owen beamed up at him. Lydia grabbed a platter of pancakes, handed Mattie the pot of *kaffi*, and they both joined the small, waiting crowd.

After silent prayer and hearty appetites had been appeased, Mattie learned the Yoder routine varied slightly from the Bellers'. Lydia gathered the empty plates. When Mattie rose to assist, Lydia shook her head. Odd. Mattie sat back down, and in a short moment, Lydia returned to be seated as well. Joel opened a Bible.

"My turn to pick a song. Right, Yo-yo?" Nine-year-old Samy spoke well with speech therapy but never dropped the pet name she used for Joel before her adoption.

Joel smiled, evidence he relished the term. "What would you like for us to sing this morning, *Leeb?*"

The girl brightened at her father's endearment. "'*Stille Nacht.*' We are learning the English. And no school today." She turned her attention in Mattie's direction, her eyes pleading.

"I started teaching the Christmas carol to them yesterday to sing for the program." She spoke to Joel but felt Winston's gaze. She didn't dare look at him. He must have heard her singing last night to chase away her fear, although he'd not mentioned a word about it. If she looked and saw him laughing at her . . .

"I'd enjoy that very much, Mattie." Winston's boldness stunned her. Finally, she looked up at him. He held her gaze, as if he desired to send her the same strength his voice possessed.

Joel cleared his throat. He glanced at Lydia first. His mouth twitched into a half-grin; then he turned to Mattie. "*Goot.* You'll lead us in singing 'Silent Night.'" He nodded.

There'd been no real question, only an understanding.

She was to begin.

If Winston had his way, he'd be listening to Mattie's melodious voice every day for the rest of his life. He'd grown to appreciate this habit of the Yoder family. Maybe he and Mattie would follow their example and do the same in their home.

With their children.

His heart hammered in his chest. His desires were running so far ahead of his reality, he wasn't sure he'd be able to catch up to make them come true.

Samy and Owen asked to be excused from the table. Maybe this was his time to get started?

"Before everyone goes along with their business, I was hoping to have a word," Winston blurted out before thinking about what would come next.

Mattie was half-standing and froze.

Joel leaned back in his chair. He stretched and then relaxed with his two hands entwined behind his head. "Don't believe anyone's going far."

"The dishes can wait." Lydia placed a hand on Mattie's shoulder, so that she sat back down. "We're all ears."

Where was he to begin?

"When I got back to Lancaster, I thought I might have to stay, at least for a little while. Turns out, Ellen's *mamm* sent her straightaway to another relative in Ohio, so I was no longer any use to help my cousin in her, uh, predicament."

Mattie's expression was the only one that held any question, but she pressed her lips together. He loved that about her. She was curious but too respectful of her friend's privacy to pry.

"On the trip home, I had time to think and pray over what I intend to do about joining the church." He heard a short gasp. Mattie's rounded eyes revealed where the surprise had landed. "I'm sorry I never had the chance to explain to you, Mattie. We got interrupted, I guess you could say, before I was able to follow through on all the things I wanted to tell you."

She nodded, as if he should go on. Lydia appeared sympathetic, while her husband had changed from amused to serious. And rightly so. It was the minister to whom he was about to speak.

"I put off joining the church at Millers Creek. Never because I doubted the call to be true to my Amish heritage, but because I had no peace about spending my life in that district. I thought my parents sent me here to get the idea of joining the New Hope district out of my head. Turns out, they understood my heart better than I realized. And as soon as I told them about . . . "

Mattie. He'd told them he'd found the woman he wanted to marry. And now, he'd backed himself into a corner. He wasn't prepared to share his intention with the whole room before he'd told her himself.

"Told them what?" Her sweet voice was barely stronger than a whisper. Would she see his silent plea, promising to tell her when they were alone?

"I explained to them why I belong here. They agreed, and my *datt* arranged for one of his truckers to drive me back through the night in order to get ahead of this storm." He turned his full attention to Joel. "I placed my faith in Jesus Christ years ago in a Mennonite revival service on a business trip. I was born again into God's family, but I need to be baptized. I am asking you to baptize me and allow me to join the New Hope church. I believe this is where God wants me to work and serve . . . and love."

The quietness of the room left him listening to the beat of his heart.

Finally, Joel answered. "I will consult with the bishop and the deacons. Until then, we will pray for *Gott's* people to understand His will in this matter when the time comes to decide. *Ya?*"

"*Ya.*" Mattie drew his attention. He glimpsed a new strength of will in the earnest focus of her storm-blue eyes. "I will pray."

Could she guess how much he hoped her future would one day be tied to those very prayers?

He couldn't tell her—even if their kissing had pretty well summed it all up. *Nay*, he had to hold his peace until he knew for sure what he could offer her.

CHAPTER FOURTEEN

A buggy, a horse, a farm, a decent living—the list of things Winston needed to begin a new life on the island seemed to grow every time he'd pondered it since the storm. He'd borrowed Joel's wagon, yet again, to take Mattie home, since the plows had finally been able to reach their road.

She sat beside him, bundled safely against the cold. He had chosen the wagon instead of the enclosed buggy, so he could hitch up the two heavy Percherons. It was the coldest but safest option for the conditions.

He moved the reins to his left hand and held out his right to Mattie. "You can scoot over closer, if you'd like." She slid over, and he pulled her into his side. "I like this much better."

She laughed. "Me, too."

He focused on driving the team. Their steady hooves drummed in rhythm to each other. Proposing to Mattie was ever on his mind. As an Amishman, he was accustomed to the need for patience. Still, being so close to her over the past day and a half was a whole other kind of waiting. He hadn't so much as stolen the smallest kiss from her while she'd been snowed in with him at the Yoders'. He'd been tempted all right. Only, he didn't imagine there was such a thing as a little kiss with Mattie right now.

More than a few times, he'd had to recall *Gott's* promise to renew the strength of those who wait on Him. Scripture likened the desired end to mounting up on wings as eagles. He expected he'd feel like he was flying if Mattie became his wife.

"What are you thinking?" Mattie's head was turned, looking up at his side profile.

"That verse from Isaiah. The one about waiting on the Lord and soaring like eagles."

"It is a beautiful promise." She stared straight ahead, as if her thoughts lay far in the distance. "I think," she looked back up at him, "our little church will welcome you, Winston. You needn't worry on it, over much."

"*Danki* for believing so." He gave her a quick squeeze, which she answered by laying her head on his shoulder. It was like her to think of him, while he'd really been thinking about her. "It also says, 'They shall run and not be weary; and they shall walk, and not faint.'[10] That's a special promise, too, isn't it, Mattie?"

"*Ya*, it surely is." She snuggled so close, Winston thought his heart might fall straight out of his ribcage.

Dear Gott, let Mattie and I soar together one day. One day soon would be real nice.

After he got her home, he'd be on his way to David Friesen's barn to check out a used buggy. If he and David worked out a deal, he'd head over to a horse farm in Cardigan to see a mare for sale.

He couldn't remain at the Yoders' forever. They'd been gracious and hospitable, but he was a visitor, not family. And as much as he hoped to be church family soon, purchasing a horse and buggy—let alone a farm—was a leap of faith. But with Mattie in his arms, big dreams seemed possible.

---

10 Isaiah 40:31

Later, he'd go finish digging out the schoolhouse, so the students could attend tomorrow and prepare for their presentation in the evening. Hopefully, he'd have a buggy of his own to drive Mattie to the Christmas Eve program—her first as the teacher.

The thought made him smile. The way the children spoke of her first day at school, he knew she was an exceptional teacher.

Too soon, they were turning into the Bellers' lane. Wide tracks marked the way where milk trucks had packed a path to the dairy between walls of snow, no doubt shoveled by Mattie's brothers.

"Would you like a ride to school tomorrow? I can come get you."

"That is very nice of you." She moved her head from his shoulder. "But I'm afraid it will require you to get up too early."

Winston laughed. "Too early for an Amishman?"

He was teasing; however, she slid out from under his arm, creating a gap between them that was anything but funny.

"I can't be certain how many parents will send their children tomorrow. We may get to have only a short rehearsal beforehand. So, there's no reason to plan on picking me up like you offered either. I don't have any idea how it will all work out."

He tried to ignore the disappointment and the doubt nagging his thoughts about her refusal of a ride. One way or another, he'd be waiting to give her a ride home after the Christmas Eve presentation.

For a reason he couldn't fathom, she became despondent whenever the subject of the school arose. Yesterday, in the matter of a single conversation, she'd transitioned from an expression of joy in the telling of her day with the children to a quiet sadness. He supposed the storm had ruined the memory. So, the sooner she got back to creating new ones was for the best.

He'd shovel the entire schoolyard himself, if necessary, to get her back to the work which made her so happy.

Mattie hurried down from the buggy before Winston could help her—before his kindness and warm touch ruined her resolve to remain true to her decision to teach the children. One more kiss and she'd be *goot* for nothing but thinking of the next one.

"*Danki.*" She called over her shoulder and scurried down the narrow pathway through the snow to her house.

Supposing her dream came true and Winston wanted her to be his *fraw*, wouldn't she be expected to give up her role as a teacher? Just when she knew *Gott* had placed in her heart to fill this need in her community. *Ach*, what a fickle thing—her heart.

Behind her, the sound of the wagon and Winston's leaving faded.

While Mattie had been gone, her *datt* must have kept the boys out of their *mamm's* way with a shovel. More pathways than usual crisscrossed over the distance between the house and the outbuildings. What appeared to be a collapsed snow tunnel began at the porch and wrapped around to the kitchen door. She hurried through the front door. She'd never been gone from home for so long and was eager to see all of them.

The living room was empty. "*Halloo!*"

She headed toward the kitchen in the eerie silence. There on the floor, her mother was knelt in prayer with her hands in front of her face. Slowly, Mattie knelt beside her, hesitant to interrupt; but she'd never seen her mother pray at this time of day. Not here—on her knees.

"*Mamm?*"

"Oh, Mattie." *Mamm* pulled her apron over her face and began to weep, her cry muffled by her hands and the fabric. "What will become of my firstborn son? What did I do wrong?"

Mattie wrapped an arm around her mother. "I've been praying he would change his mind. We'll get through this. We will."

Her mother dropped the apron and stared at her. Her eyes were red with dark half-moons under each one, as if she hadn't slept well for days. "You knew?"

"I . . . "

"You knew your brother ran off to join the military, and you didn't tell me? Oh, daughter, how could you?"

"*Nay*! *Mamm*, he did not tell me this part. Only . . . " What had her brother said exactly? "He said he had a job. That Ellen wasn't the right woman for him . . . or something like that." She sucked in a breath, then rummaged in her pocket for her inhaler. "What did you say about the military? I don't understand. Are you sure?"

Mattie inhaled the blessed steroid to help her breath and counted to ten. "They can't force him to join. *Datt* and the bishop will go and explain. Mark has been upset. He just made a mistake."

"*Nay*, Mattie. He will not change his mind. He is determined to do this abomination. To his faith. To his people. To *Gott*." *Mamm* lifted the apron to cover her face again. She rocked back and forth. "He thinks he can save lives with his brain for numbers. How has the devil deceived my child so?"

But Mark had not joined the church or taken a vow of non-violence,, so he would not be shunned; for that, Mattie was grateful. Still, she held her peace. None of her words would comfort her mother right now. And no platitudes existed to console such grief. Instead, she remained prostrate alongside her beloved *mamm* and prayed in silence for the comfort of *Gott's* Holy Spirit to ease their pain.

What in the world was Mark thinking? What a lonesome road her dear, brave brother had chosen in doing what he believed to be right.

She would pray for him every day, no matter how her own heart ached at his choice. Her own crossroad loomed ahead. One way led to Winston—the other to a one-room schoolhouse. How had her simple life become so complicated so quickly?

CHAPTER FIFTEEN

As Winston drove up to the school at dusk on Christmas Eve, he was hard-pressed to reconcile the view as the same one where he'd found Mattie hiding under her desk three days ago.

Joel's neighbor, Dan King, had kindly bulldozed the lot to provide parking. Buggies, plus a few cars belonging to some *Englisch* guests, formed a line in front of a steep wall of snow. Candles flickered in the windows, illuminating paper snowflakes on the higher panes. Excited chatter met him at the door. The noise was joyful, full of eagerness for the district's first Christmas with a school. And yet, he much preferred the quietness which had carried Mattie's melody to him through the snowy night.

He stepped through the door and shuffled a short way to the right, staying close to the back wall. The room was instinctually divided with men on the right side of the back entrance and women to the left, the same as during worship services. They sat on church benches, which had been brought in to accommodate the extra crowd.

Unlike a Sunday service, the children occupied the front rows in their school desks, while the adults sat behind them on the bench seats. Some of the non-Amish guests stood, as he did, against the back wall. A few others had assimilated in among the men and women, as if the gender division was their normal way. He knew it was not and appreciated their courtesy.

And then, he saw her. Mattie stood in the center aisle between the rows of her students—a silhouette in the dim background against the more brightly lit front of the room.

She bent to speak into her brother Michael's ear. He stood and led a procession of the children to the front of the room, where they turned to face the crowd. A hush fell across the room.

This was the one and only time in the year when the Amish approved of a performance. No other time would the children be the center of attention on a stage—only when they presented their learning in honor of the birth of Jesus.

Stille nacht . . .

In unison, their voices raised the German Christmas hymn to the ears of their parents, aunts, uncles, and even neighbors. Soon, a hum buzzed in the crowd. How the Amish loved to sing. Before long, a few others hummed along, still cautious not to overpower the children's voices.

Winston remembered Mattie's plan to have them sing in English. Sure enough, when the last German verse ended, they switched. As the first silent night filled the air, approving nods rippled through the audience. Teaching English was one of the most important goals of the school.

Mattie knew what she was doing. And she'd only just begun.

When the song ended, one lonely clap snapped through the silence, likely from an *Englischer* who didn't realize he'd be alone. The children returned to their desks. Their faces beamed. They'd witnessed the approval of their families in the nods and the hums. They'd never expect applause.

The smile stretching across Winston's face was full of pride in the woman he loved. He knew so. But heaven help him if he could do anything about it.

As the children came back to their seats, Mattie stood in the center aisle. On a long breath to ease her anxiety, she offered a silent prayer of thankfulness for the darkness. If Winston had come, she hadn't seen him yet. If she saw him now, her concentration might take flight. She kept her focus to the front benches, where the elderly and parents with small children were seated.

Rather than stand at the front of the room, she stopped in the aisle, a spot close to the position the minister would take on a Sunday morning. The weight of unworthiness kept her feet planted in place a few seconds longer. At least they never met for church in the school-house—some comfort.

She turned. A room full of people waited.

"Thank you to everyone who has come to our program tonight." The rehearsed words began to flow more easily. "You will be seeing and hearing from each child tonight—some individually, others by grade, but all to represent their work so far this year. In her absence, we wish to sincerely thank Ellen Miller, the teacher who taught the children so well this term." Out of habit, she dropped her head, ever so slightly, in a sign of respect to those listening.

Her lowered eyes caught her father watching from the first bench to her left. He shared an understanding nod as their eyes met.

No matter Ellen's cause to leave, she had done the work to make this night possible. *Datt* had agreed, even if others may not. The bond with her father was powerful *goot* to her heart in a moment like this. She took her seat with a far lighter load on her shoulders.

The three oldest girls made their way up front to recite the first chapter of Luke from memory. She smiled at them, hoping to be an encouragement. She could rest easy for now. She didn't have to speak again until the end.

Then she'd have to face Winston. Unless he hadn't come at all, since she'd refused his invitation to bring her. As much as she missed him and wanted to see him again, things might be for the better if he hadn't come tonight.

All the children gave their best efforts in doing their parts. Mattie praised them in front of their families, then invited everyone to enjoy refreshments before leaving.

The gas lanterns were turned high to brighten the whole room, as folks made their way to the sweets—cookies and fruit punch—on a table along the wall where the women had been seated. The room was crowded, although the boys had followed her instructions to move benches to the far wall and take the rest back outside to the church wagon.

A tingling sensation made her turn around to see who was watching her.

Winston.

He stood in the far corner. His gaze was intense and directed at her. He smiled, the one that melted her insides, then lifted a cup to his lips and drained the pink drink. He didn't appear to be going anywhere, no matter how much she avoided him.

132   THE *Christmas* VISITOR

Mark walked up to him, drawing his attention off her. Quickly, she returned to the far side of the room and busied herself with serving seconds.

She searched for every empty-handed guest available to keep her distracted.

"Mattie." She jumped at the familiar voice behind her. "Will you ignore me forever?"

She shuffled the cookies back to the center of the tray, then turned to face him, wishing she could act innocent. She could not. She loved this man. And when she glimpsed such tenderness from him suggesting he might love her . . .

Ach, but she loved being a teacher, too. Maybe not in the same way, but she'd made a commitment. And teaching was a talent she could finally invest for the Lord and His Kingdom.

Why did all this *wunderbaar* goodness have to happen all at once? Why couldn't it be spread across a lifetime, so she wouldn't have to choose?

"What's the matter? You can share anything with me, Mattie. Anything." He reached out a hand, then withdrew before touching her cheek. "Not here." He looked over her shoulder, then back to her. "I bought a horse and buggy today. I'll wait for you."

She blinked, and he was gone. Someone else was asking her when school was going to go back to regular hours after Christmas on a Friday. "On Monday. Like usual."

She tried to smile. Only nothing was usual at all anymore.

She hadn't answered Winston. She'd been too stunned. He'd bought a horse and buggy. Here on the island? So, he meant to stay.

The conclusion made her heart thud so hard, she hadn't been able to respond. Now, he'd walked away.

A half-hour later, she slipped out of the school, leaving only her *datt* and Bishop Nafziger still talking in low voices. Everyone else had already left.

The cold air revived her after so long in an overcrowded room. The downhill walk home would do her good.

She stepped off the porch and caught sight of Winston around the corner.

He leaned against the second-to-last buggy in the lot. His buggy. The other was her father's. She supposed her *datt* would take the bishop home but wondered if *Mamm* and the boys had walked home without him. Dear, sweet *Mamm*. *Help her, Gott.*

"Dan King gave them a ride in his van."

Did Winston always find her so transparent? She hoped not. A person liked some privacy of thought.

"And I'm not about to freeze while waiting on the bishop, you know." He opened the buggy door. "Only for you."

She remembered then what he'd said after the part about buying a horse and buggy, which was the same as saying he was staying for good. He'd wait for her.

Against all her *goot* sense, she slid into the front seat of Winston's buggy, carrying the heat of his stare with her. She had to get this over and done with and tell him why she couldn't spend time with him anymore.

Would he understand? Maybe give her a final goodbye kiss?

Nay. Not a sensible idea, at all. She wished it all the same.

He slipped into the seat beside her and closed the door before wrapping a heavy blanket over them. Then, her toe bumped a warm coal box. "I used some hot coals from the woodstove to fill it up."

"*Danki.*" Her feet would be toasty warm all the way home.

"I do have a courting buggy at home. At home in Lancaster, I mean. And I will make arrangements to bring things here, as soon as I have my own place. But for now, this buggy and horse were *Gott's* provision." Winston reached for her hand, but she slipped it just beneath her woolen cape. "The deacons have agreed to bring my membership and baptism before the church, as long as I meet with Joel and the bishop to understand and agree with the doctrine and *Ordnung* here." He turned the horse onto the quiet road and eased her forward in a slow and steady walk. "I believe you know what all this means . . . for us."

Did she? Right now, she was jealous of whoever had ridden with him in that courting buggy in Pennsylvania. Regardless, she knew what she must say. Soon, before she lost the chance. "I'll never regret our time together. Or the . . . well, how special it has been."

"Kissing, you mean. 'Cause, I can't forget it. Don't plan to either." A new tension entered his voice.

She didn't like the sound and must be going at this all wrong. "I don't believe *Gott* would have me give up teaching. I just started. It would upset the children again. And . . . and it would upset me."

Icy snow crunched under the wheels. Minute after long minute, the horses' clip carried them ever closer to home. By the time they turned into the Bellers' lane, she had to keep her mittens against her face to absorb the tears she couldn't contain.

As soon as the buggy stopped, she'd run and never look back.

Winston halted the horse in front of the house. Her fingers fumbled for the latch to escape the buggy, but Winston's strong arms wrapped around her and hugged her into his chest.

"Oh, Mattie, *mei leeb*. I would never." He loosened his hold, and she pulled back to see his face in the moonlight. He removed his gloves and thumbed away the tears on her cheeks. "I would never take away anything that gives you purpose in serving *Gott* or our people. I promise."

She saw pain on his face, like a mirror of the deep hurt she felt and he now soothed. Had she offended him? "I did not think badly of you. I only thought . . . well, I didn't really dare to think too much about it at all."

"I haven't been able to think of much else. Only *Gott* can see so far into the future. He knows what decisions we will face along the road ahead of us. Just like He has shown you what you must do now in serving Him and the community, He will provide us with direction when—or if—He blesses us with a family of our own. He always makes a way to do what is right in every situation." He reached for her hand. "You're cold. We should go inside to finish talking."

"All right then." The short reply was all she could muster.

Little wonder. Her heart had stopped a minute ago. She needed to go inside to absorb what he'd promised. Did it change anything? Everything?

In her *mamm's* kitchen, they warmed by the stove. Mattie heated a kettle to make some hot peppermint and chamomile tea. She heard her *datt* come in the front door. His steps headed directly toward the other side of the house, and then her parents' bedroom door squeaked shut.

One sign among many indicating his worry about his *fraw*. He'd pay extra careful consideration to her through this difficult time; her *datt* always took care of her *mamm*.

Winston leaned back in the chair he'd pulled from the table to get closer to the heat. The kitchen was more than warm already. "Mark asked for Ellen's new address."

Mattie got up from the chair beside him to pour the hot water and steep the tea. "I suppose you've heard what he's done."

"*Ya*." His voice was solemn behind her. "And you know about Ellen, then?"

"From my *mamm*," she answered without turning to look back at him. Grateful for busy hands to avoid more details, she rummaged through the drawer for a spoon. "In spite of all that, Mark would still want to make sure she's all right. He sold his car to give her money. He must care for her."

"Oh. I has no idea, Ellen didn't tell me that." Winston's chair skooched against the floor. With a side-glance she saw him walking toward the cabinet where she was stretching for the honey to sweeten the tea. He reached over her, easily retrieving the jar. "I might have misjudged your brother. If you think I should, then I will ask her permission to give Mark her address." He was standing very close. The warmth of his breath tickled the back of her neck. "Whatever you think, *mei leeb*."

Her hands trembled, so that the teaspoon clattered into the cup. "*Ya*, that's a *goot* way to handle it." She tried to pull herself together before turning around with two steaming cups of tea.

"Let me help." Winston carried the cups and set them on the table. "I need your advice on something else, too." Before she could sit, he stepped in front of her and took both of her hands in his. He ran his thumb across her wrist and then lifted his golden-brown eyes to her face. "A man needs land to make a home with the woman he wants to become . . . his family." He stalled on the last two words, sending a thrill all the way to her toes. His lips twitched upward with that cheeky grin she'd come to adore.

She pulled her hands out of his. "It's almost too warm in here, don't you think?" She smoothed her frizzing curls back from her forehead toward her *kapp.*

"You're not helping, *Leeb.*"

What? She let out a frustrated puff to blow the curls back.

"That's not what I meant." That infuriating grin of his grew more . . . more . . . charming.

Oh, understanding bloomed. Men were strange creatures. She put on her best unaffected front. "And you were saying?"

He cleared his throat. "And . . . I've had a hobby of learning about trees. Being a salesman in the building business started it, I guess. Anyway, I'd make a poor dairy farmer. But a maple tree farm . . . I'd do well in that kind of business."

She studied him and agreed. He suited the life, at least in the way she imagined it. Tending trees, making and selling syrup, a nice homey business on a farm attracting tourists and locals. She'd crunch all the numbers. *Ach,* what an imagination. She reined her thoughts back to the here and now. "I believe you might have come to the right place, then."

"*Ya,* I believe I have." His amber eyes shimmered. "Thing is, I'm going to need the best spot around to get started on growing a tree stand for a future business And I have it on *goot* authority that you,

Mattie Beller, have a keen sense for directing a man to purchase just the right land to meet his needs."

"Who told you so?"

"Your *datt* told me the very first day I met you. You're not going to tell me he was just matchmaking, are you?"

"Nay." On second thought, maybe *Datt* had been looking out for her, yet again. "I do have a bit of a gift with maps and numbers. I might be persuaded to use them in your favor. And I do love maple trees. I also love . . . the syrup, too."

His laughter echoed with delight. And the pieces of her heart, fractured by their earlier misunderstanding, began to meld. He stepped closer and pulled her hands to him. "Either way, makes no matter. I've discovered plenty of reasons to love you."

"Are you proposing just to get me to find you a perfect farm?" She teased, unsure how far to allow her heart to take Winston's meaning. She believed the promise he'd made to her in the buggy. And in it, she felt free to answer both calls of her heart. To teach as long as *Gott* had need for her. And the other . . .

The warmth of his hands moved higher to her shoulders. His touch firm, yet kind, entreating her to hear him. As if he didn't already have every nervous strand of her undivided attention.

"*Ya*, I am, Mattie Beller. And then, I'm gonna marry you just so I can keep on loving the woman who made all my dreams come true." His gaze intensified. "For the rest of my life."

Mattie's heart pounded. Her face flushed with heat.

The man she'd grown to love and trust, who cherished her and believed in her, held her gaze until his assurance penetrated to the deepest part of her soul. "So, what do you say? I love you, Mattie. Will you marry me?"

If a yes could be stated in a kiss, then she must have gotten the answer exactly right because Winston scooped her up and whooped until she was sure the whole house would come running to put out the fire.

THE END

A Canadian Amish farmer
A Lancaster Amish businesswoman
A Prince Edward Island foster child

Amish Dreams on Prince Edward Island
Book One

FOREVER *Home*

AMY GROCHOWSKI

Providence brings together a mismatched family, giving all three a second chance for love. Only love may never have had such a tough job.

Lydia Miller is an anomaly among her Amish people—a single woman in her 30s, running her own store, determined to forge a life on her own. But when Joel Yoder comes into town to sell his property, Lydia suddenly finds all of her hopes and dreams crumbling around her and a new opportunity placed in her lap.

Joel has his own problems. Recently jilted by his fiancée, Joel has seen his own dreams of moving to a newly established Amish community begin to falter. The new community welcomes married couples only. With his dreams quickly slipping from his fingers, Joel suddenly sees the only option he thinks he has-a marriage of convenience for both of them.

As the new couple begins life in a new settlement, they are even more surprised when a foster child in need of a home finds her way to them. Yet what will happen when the English world and the Amish world collide?

Dear Readers,

Thank you for following along with Mattie and Winston in the continuing story of the fictional Amish community on Prince Edward Island. While the New Hope community setting, church, and all of the characters are fictional, I have done my best to create a fair representation of the life and faith of the Canadian Amish in the Maritimes.

I'd like to thank the many sources who helped me in the details of this story, including the friendly PEI Snowmobile Association Facebook groups for allowing me to listen and learn from them. Any and all mistakes are my own.

A huge debt of gratitude belongs to my family, friends, and Word Weaver pals who support me as I spend hours cloistered away to write. Mom and Kim, thank you for all the days you made sure I got much-needed quiet time. Mattie and Winston's story wouldn't exist without you—or my amazing critique partner, Laurel Blount, who blesses me beyond words.

David, my love, any spark of romance has your inspiration written all over it.

Most of all, thanks be to the Lord, who continues to bless me with the joy of creating new stories for you to read. I hope you will find His love written into the pages here.

As always, feel free to email me at amygrocho.author@gmail.com. For more books in this series, you may wish to visit my website at www.amygrochoski.com.

Until then, I'll be writing the next happily forever after, coming soon.

Much Love and Appreciation,

Amy Grochowski

For more information about
Amy Grochowski
&
The Christmas Visitor
please visit:

www.amygrochowski.com
www.facebook.com/amygrochowski
www.instagram.com/AmyGrocho
www.goodreads.com/amygrocho
@AmyGrocho

For more information about
AMBASSADOR INTERNATIONAL
please visit:

www.ambassador-international.com
@AmbassadorIntl
www.facebook.com/AmbassadorIntl

If you enjoyed this book, please consider leaving us a review on
Amazon, Goodreads, or our website.

More from Ambassador International

Abigail Walker is on the cusp of womanhood. Awkward and unsure of herself, Abby is flustered when she meets Harvey Nicholas, the nephew of a family at her church. As summer begins, Abby finds herself constantly in the company of Harvey and falling quickly in love with him. But will Abby and Harvey's love be able to withstand distance, rumors, loss, and hurt? Or will the war be what tears apart Abby's heart?

War-Torn Heart
by Allison Wells

Evie Parker is plagued by a recurring nightmare from her childhood—who is the woman in her dream? What does it mean? A deathbed confession compels Evie to leave her home in Rhode Island and travel to the Territory of Alaska, where she struggles to unravel a past shrouded in mystery. Can she come through storms, both physical and emotional, to open her heart to true love?

Till the Storm Passes By

by AnnaLee Conti

Computer expert Lexi Wynn is frightened. Someone is after her, but she doesn't know why. Escaping a failed kidnapping attempt and not sure who to trust, she hopes her specialized skills with computers might flush out the name of the killer. When a tall, dark, and handsome stranger rams into her truck with the hearse he's driving and puts his life in danger to save hers, can she ignore the attraction she feels for him to concentrate on the killers? Or is God the only one who can save her now?

Murder for the Time Being

by Joanie Bruce